Bidu's Adventures
Fairy Beginnings

Denise Ganulin

Grosvenor House
Publishing Limited

This book is published by
Grosvenor House Publishing Ltd
Link House
140 The Broadway, Tolworth, Surrey, KT6 7HT.
www.grosvenorhousepublishing.co.uk

A CIP record for this book
is available from the British Library

ISBN 978-1-83975-722-8

To Bidu, my amazing granddaughter,
without whom this book would
never have been written.
Your ideas and imagination are in every chapter,
your beautiful heart and kindness on every page.
Your sweet love is a precious, treasured gift. What
a joy it is to be your 'Moni'! Near or far, you are
always in my heart. You make the world a
brighter place just by being YOU. May your life
be filled with many wonderful adventures.
May your every dream come true.

Table Of Contents

1

Fairies are real!

It was a beautiful sunny day, one of those days with just a little breeze, a clear blue sky and lots of the exciting sounds of nature. It was just the kind of day that made Bidu (*Bee-doo*) happy. In fact, it was the kind of day that could make almost anyone happy!

Bidu was a sweet 11-year-old girl who lived in Mayville, a small town with big hearted people just like her. She didn't have any brothers or sisters, so she found wonderful things to do on her own. Her favorite time was being outdoors with nature. Bidu especially loved to climb up the big hill behind her house. She loved to go way up to the very top where there were lots of butterflies and birds and flowers. The butterflies would fly to her, surrounding her as she sang songs to them. Sometimes she would take her recorder and play music as the butterflies and birds flew all around while she danced with them. Bidu liked to spread her arms out so the butterflies could land on her and then she would softly sing to them and watch them flap their wings. They were so beautiful with their bright, vibrant colors and they never seemed to be afraid of her. It was like they could sense her gentleness and they seemed to feel her amazing love for them.

Bidu loved sitting for hours just to watch the clouds go by. She loved to see the many wonderful shapes they made. She could see so many things in the clouds and she would make up stories with every different shape that went by. Sometimes she would lie down on her back to watch the birds fly above her as she wondered what it would be like to fly with them. She secretly wished she really could fly way up in the sky. She would imagine soaring and floating in the wind.

All of the birds and butterflies loved it when Bidu came running up the hill. They waited for her to come every day. On the days Bidu couldn't come, they were sad. It just wasn't the same without her visit. She loved them so much and they loved her too. She was their best friend and every day they watched for her to come up the hill as they listened for her songs. Sometimes they would make a little nest of flowers for her because they were so happy she came to see them. Bidu would bring bits of bread from home and she would always make sure that every bird got a bite.

One Saturday, when Bidu was running up the hill, she heard an unusual sound. It was a sound she had never heard before. She knew most of the bird sounds, and she could even recognize some of the butterflies from the way they flapped their wings. But this sound was different. She couldn't tell where it was coming from at first, but some of the butterflies started to fly around one of the big trees. Bidu thought they were signaling something to her so she went to see what was there.

She was so surprised, because right there, at the bottom of the tree, in a big patch of grass was what looked like a little fairy. Bidu couldn't believe her eyes. She believed in fairies but she had never seen one in person before. She slowly moved closer so as not to scare her. She looked down at the little creature and softly said, "Are you a fairy?"

The fairy looked scared. "Yes," she said, "I am."

"Don't be afraid, little fairy," said Bidu softly. "I won't hurt you. Are you all right?"

The fairy looked up at Bidu with loving eyes and said, "I am lost. I was out flying when I saw all of these beautiful butterflies. I stopped paying attention to where I was going and I bumped into the tree. My left wing is hurt. I can't fly."

The fairy started to cry. Bidu gently lifted her from the ground and cradled her in her hands. "Don't worry, little fairy," she said. "I will help you."

Bidu wasn't sure what she should do to help the fairy, but she knew she had to do something to wrap the fairy's wing so it could rest. The birds were very good at gathering string for their nests, so Bidu asked them to find their strongest, but softest pieces of string.

The birds flew off in search of the string while Bidu stayed with the fairy who was crying because she missed her home and she was scared. She was worried about the other fairies who did not know where she was, especially her mother and father.

Bidu tried to reassure her. "Don't worry, little fairy. I will take care of you until your wing is healed and then I will help you find the other fairies. Maybe they are out looking for you right now." Bidu tried to make her feel better and the fairy was happy she was there with her.

"I heard you singing to the butterflies," the fairy said. "Would you please sing to me?"

"Of course I will," said Bidu. She gently placed the fairy in her lap as she started to sing sweet little songs. The fairy cuddled up and was very happy she had a friend to help her. She could tell there was something special about Bidu. She could feel her love and she felt safe.

While they were waiting for the birds to return, Bidu talked to the fairy trying to help keep her calm. There were so many questions she wanted to ask, so many things she wanted to know.

"Do fairies have names?" asked Bidu.

"Yes. My name is Pirube (*Pie-Ruby*). What is your name?" asked the fairy.

"My name is Bidu."

"That is a very sweet name," said Pirube. "You know, we will be friends forever because you have saved me and helped me and made me feel better. I will teach you special things about fairies and magic. One day when I am better, I will take you to my land."

"Oh, I want to know all about your land and what it's like to be a real fairy," cried Bidu. "Can you really do magic?"

"You will see for yourself," said Pirube smiling. "I can show you many things."

"That would be so wonderful!" exclaimed Bidu.

"I want to know everything about being a little girl, too," said Pirube.

"You know, all fairies would like to know humans, but not all humans believe we are real."

"Oh Pirube, I have always believed fairies are real!" Bidu said excitedly. "I want to know everything about you, and I will tell you and show you everything about my world too."

Soon the birds began to come back with lots of string. Blue, pink, red, purple… so many colors. Bidu knew how to make a braid so she took all the pieces of string and braided them together until they made a beautiful rainbow sling to hold the fairy's sore wing. The little fairy felt so much better, but she could not move her wing and she wondered if she would ever be able to fly again.

"We will need to start heading down the hill soon," said Bidu.

The fairy could not fly and she didn't want to be left alone, so Bidu asked Pirube to go home with her where she could stay for the night. Then, tomorrow in the daylight she would bring her back up the hill.

"Tomorrow is Sunday," said Bidu. "There is no school, so I can stay with you and we can search for your family."

The fairy was so happy to have a friend. She just knew that if she were with Bidu, she would stay safe.

Bidu started thinking. She still had so many more questions for the fairy.

"Do fairies have families?"

"Yes, of course," said the fairy. "We have very big families. I will take you to meet them. They will be happy to meet you and you will love them all!"

Bidu was so interested in everything Pirube was saying that she didn't notice the sun setting. She was never late for dinner and she didn't want to disappoint her parents.

"We need to go now, so I'm not late," Bidu said.

They started down the hill, but Bidu was still talking. "I wonder what fairies eat for dinner?" she asked.

Pirube laughed to herself because fairies don't eat what little girls eat. They just breathe in the beautiful air and make fairy dust. Then they eat the fairy dust which gives them the energy to fly.

Bidu wasn't the only one with questions. The fairy had lots of questions about being a little girl. But for now, Pirube just tried to lie still as Bidu carried her down the hill.

It was getting dark now. Bidu tried to hurry, but not so fast as to move Pirube too much. She knew her wing must be hurting, so she tried to be as gentle as possible with every step. Pirube knew how careful Bidu was trying to be so she laid as still as she could.

Bidu couldn't wait to show the fairy everything about her life and she certainly wanted to know everything about Pirube's life. Up until now, Bidu had only dreamed about fairies and what they might be like. Now she was holding one! She couldn't believe it, but here she was doing it.

Pirube had always wondered about the human world and now here she was with who she was sure was the sweetest girl in the world. They were both in awe and wonder!

Even though they were both surprised to have met each other, and they had no idea of what was about to happen, somehow they were sure they were going to have an amazing friendship and even more amazing adventures together.

2

Fairy Lessons

It was almost completely dark as Bidu approached her house. She could hear her mother calling her name.

"Bidu!" she cried. "Bidu, where are you?"

"Here I am, Mama," Bidu yelled. She could see her mother and she didn't look happy.

"I was so worried," she said. "It's not like you to be late for dinner. Are you all right?"

"Yes," said Bidu. "I'm so sorry I made you worry."

"I'm just glad you're here now," said her mother. "How about you go and get cleaned up for dinner? I made your favorite tonight, chicken and noodles."

Bidu smiled. "I'm so hungry! I'll be right there."

Bidu took Pirube into her bedroom. She carefully placed her in one of her shoe boxes. She laid some pieces of fabric on the bottom so that it would be soft and comfortable.

She told Pirube, "I will not tell my parents about you just yet, so you stay here and rest. Can I bring you anything?"

Pirube said, "No, sweet Bidu, I'll be fine. I'm very tired and my wing hurts, so I'll just try to lay still and rest. You go and have a nice dinner. I'll be waiting for you to return."

Bidu blew her a kiss as she went to have dinner. She loved her mama's chicken and noodles and she was really hungry tonight. She felt bad that she had worried her parents. She wanted so much to tell them about the fairy, but didn't want to just blurt it out, so she decided to wait until later.

When she went into the kitchen, her father said, "Bidu, you know how much we love you. We let you go up the hill by yourself because you are so responsible and trustworthy. You always come home before dark. What happened today?"

"Oh, Daddy, I'm so sorry. I lost track of the day, but it won't happen again, I promise." Bidu was truly sorry and her father could see that. She was always so responsible. Her father decided to let it go this time, because he believed that she would not be late again.

"OK, Bidu. I understand. There must have been a good reason. Something important must have happened. Maybe you can tell us, but first let's have a nice dinner. Your mother made your favorite for you."

Her mother filled her plate with hot chicken and noodles. Just the smell made Bidu happy. She started gobbling down her food.

Her mother laughed. "You must be very hungry to be eating so fast, but slow down so you can enjoy it. You don't have anywhere else to go."

Her parents didn't yet know about the fairy and that Bidu wanted to get back to check on her, but she slowed down so she could have a nice dinner with them. She helped with the dishes, then hurried back to her room.

Pirube was still in the box. She was awake. "Oh, Bidu, I'm so glad you're back. I was feeling scared even though I could hear you talking with your parents. I am missing my family so much."

Bidu felt so sad for Pirube. She sat down next to her and said, "I know this must be very hard for you. What can I do to make you feel better?"

Pirube looked up at Bidu. "Maybe we can try to find my home."

Bidu answered as gently as she could. "Maybe we should wait for your wing to heal."

Bidu sat up like a light bulb went on in her head. "Wait a minute!" cried Bidu. "Didn't you tell me you could do magic?"

"Yes, I can do magic," said Pirube.

"Then why can't you just make your wing better?"

"Because that would just be doing something for me," Pirube told Bidu.

"Yes," said Bidu. "But what's wrong with that?"

Pirube took a big breath and softly said, "I think it's time for me to explain fairy magic to you so that you will understand."

"Oh, I want to understand everything," Bidu said excitedly.

"Then listen carefully so I can tell you."

Bidu sat down and was very quiet. Pirube started speaking. "I can only use my magic for good, Bidu. And I can only do that good if it's for someone else. I can't just make anything happen that I want. Especially something like fixing my wing. You see, when you found me earlier, I was out following the butterflies. Like you, I always love to be with nature. My mother told me to pay attention to where I was at all times, so that I wouldn't get lost again."

"Again?" interrupted Bidu.

"Yes, again. I have been lost before, but I never hurt myself. One time my family searched all day for me. I felt terrible, just like you did tonight when you were late to dinner. It feels awful to disappoint someone you love or to make them worry, don't you agree?"

"Oh yes," said Bidu. "I felt awful too about tonight, but I don't understand why you can't just heal yourself so you can get back home."

"That's what I'm trying to explain to you, sweet girl. I went where I shouldn't have gone today. Getting lost was the consequence of that, but so was hurting my wing. You could say it was an accident, but I knew better really and I followed those beautiful butterflies anyway, without paying attention to where I was. When I am home, and I fall or hurt myself in any way, another fairy can heal me in an instant. That's because they are using their powers to help another. One of the best things about being a fairy is that I DO have the power to help others. When I use my power with that kind of good, there is no better feeling in the world."

Bidu nodded as if she understood.

Pirube continued. "Have you ever done something very special for your mother or father?"

"Oh yes," said Bidu. "It was my mama's birthday a few weeks ago and I got up early and made her breakfast in bed. When I brought it to her, she was so happy. My heart swelled with joy and love. Is that what you mean?"

"Exactly!" cried Pirube. "You understand. We fairies are small and delicate, but we are full of love that we want to share. We try to always be examples of goodness. We are happy and joyful every day because we can give to others. Right now, I cannot do something just for me. I will have to wait for my wing to heal… unless…"

"Unless what?" Bidu asked. "What are you thinking, Pirube? Please tell me!"

"Let me think for a minute, Bidu." Pirube closed her eyes like she was going into some kind of trance. Bidu sat very quietly, but inside she was praying that the answer would come.

It seemed like a long time passed, and then Pirube opened her eyes. She smiled as she spoke.

"Bidu, I think I might have a solution. A real fairy solution."

Bidu wanted to cry out, "Tell me, tell me," but instead she sat quietly, waiting for Pirube to explain.

"I want to take you to my land. You have saved me and I want to do something wonderful for you. But, if I take you as a girl, you might scare some of the fairies because you would be so big to them and they don't know you. Some of the fairies have been hurt by humans. That's why we don't show ourselves to very many. I have thought about this. I can use my power to make you become a fairy."

Bidu's eyes grew huge. "You mean, I won't be Bidu anymore?"

Pirube laughed. "Yes, you will always still be Bidu. I will only make you a fairy for a short time. Once my family gets to know you, then you can be a girl again with them and they won't be afraid of you ever. They will know and love you as I do."

Bidu still seemed worried. "I want to go to meet your family. I really do, but I can't leave here for very long because I don't want my parents to worry anymore."

Pirube smiled. "I understand. You are a sweet girl. I can see that you think of others. Just know that they won't even realize you are gone. One of my powers is that I can make time stand still. I can do this for the entire time we are gone and to this world it will be like no time has passed at all. I will do this in a very special spell that I put on your parents, so they won't have any worries."

"How exactly does that work?" Bidu wanted to know.

"Well, we will wait until your parents are sleeping. I will cast the spell and then we can go to my land. For as long as we are gone, it will still be tonight and they will still be asleep. They won't be able to wake up until you are back safely. Then it will be just like any other morning!"

Bidu had more questions. "So if you make me little, then how will I carry you? How will we know how to get to your land?"

Pirube tried to explain more. "Bidu, when I use my power to change you into a fairy, I will be doing it as a gift for you, and for my family. That is all good. Once I make you a fairy, you will have fairy powers to help others, just like I do. The first thing you could do, would be to heal my wing. Then we could fly together to my land."

Bidu asked, "But how will we find your land?"

"That's a very good question, Bidu. I will tell you," Pirube said.

"One of the wonderful things about fairy wings is that they have a built-in compass and direction finders. But if I can't fly, then those don't work. If you are a fairy and we both have wings that work, then we will find my land very easily. It shouldn't be too far away, because I wasn't really gone that long. It's just that once I hit the tree, I was instantly lost because without a wing, I no longer had the power of direction. Do you understand?"

"Yes, I think I do," said Bidu.

"Do you have any more questions for me?" asked Pirube.

Bidu thought about it. She was a little nervous about being turned into a fairy, but she was very excited about going to Pirube's land.

"I think I have a few more questions," she said.

"Well, go ahead and ask all the questions you have because I want you to be very comfortable once we get started."

Bidu felt very safe with Pirube, but still she decided to ask her questions.

"Will I feel anything when you change me into a fairy?"

"Not a thing," answered Pirube. "One minute you will be a girl, the next minute you will be a fairy. You won't feel anything. It might take a little getting used to because you will be much smaller. You will need to try out your wings before we get going, but that will be fun."

Then Bidu asked, "You will definitely be able to change me back when it's time, right?"

"In an instant!" Pirube replied.

"And my parents won't know I'm even gone?"

"Not for a minute. They will be sleeping in their bed having very sweet dreams. I'll make sure of that. Anything else?" Pirube asked.

Bidu thought for a moment. Then she said, "No, I don't think so. I think I understand everything. I guess I'm ready to go. Now what?"

Pirube smiled. She was happy that she would be going home. She was even happier that Bidu would be going with her as a fairy. She would show her so many things. She couldn't wait to go!

She looked lovingly at Bidu and said, "Go say goodnight to your parents like you do every night. Then come back here and we will wait together until they go to sleep. Once they are soundly asleep, I will cast the spell and we will go."

Bidu went into the living room where her parents were sitting and reading in front of the fire.

"I came to say goodnight," she said. "I'm pretty tired."

"OK, sweetheart," said her father. "We will come tuck you in for the night in a few minutes."

Bidu loved bedtime, because her parents always came into her room and sat on her bed and gave her big hugs and kisses. It was always a wonderful time that she looked forward to. So, off she went to brush her teeth. She put on her favorite nightgown. It was the pink one with little maroon and lavender flowers, and a crimson red butterfly on the shoulder. Pirube watched as Bidu snuggled into her bed.

A few minutes later, Bidu's parents came into the room.

"Why, you look like a little angel," her mother said as she sat on the bed and gave Bidu a long loving hug. "Have a wonderful sleep! We'll see you in the morning."

Then her daddy sat down. He always stroked her hair and face and told her how much he loved her. Then he gave her a big hug. He smiled at her as he said, "We'll see you in the morning, sweetheart." Then he left with her mother. They both turned for one more look at their precious daughter as they turned off the light and shut the door.

Pirube waited to be sure they were gone before she spoke. "Oh Bidu, you have such wonderful parents. Watching them love you like that makes me miss my family so much."

"Soon you will be back home, Pirube, and I'm so happy I will get to meet your family. So tell me now, what is going to happen?"

Pirube thought before she answered because she wanted to be sure she didn't miss anything that Bidu would need to know right now.

"First of all, once your parents are asleep, I will sprinkle them with fairy dust and put a beautiful spell on them which will allow time to stand still while they have a wonderful, peaceful sleep. They will not wake up until we are back when we can remove the spell. It must be a good spell for them so that they have no worries."

"And then will you make me into a fairy?" Bidu asked excitedly.

Pirube enjoyed Bidu's enthusiasm. She wanted this to be the most wonderful adventure for Bidu.

"Yes, Bidu. Then I will make you into a fairy!"

They waited for what seemed like a long time, but really it was only about half an hour before the house was silent and her parents were fast asleep. Pirube asked Bidu, "Would you like to come to watch me put the spell on your parents?"

"Oh yes, I want to see everything!"

"OK then, let's go quietly."

Bidu tiptoed as she carried Pirube very carefully. Pirube told her to put her down on her parents' bed.

She began to move her arms and hands in a special circular motion. All of a sudden, she was making fairy dust. It looked like golden glitter. She began to sprinkle it, but because her wing was broken, she couldn't get high enough in the air.

"Bidu, I will need you to help me. Can you please scatter the fairy dust higher up so that it will fall gently onto your parents?" Of course, Bidu was so happy to help. She had never seen fairy dust before. It was so shiny! More shiny than anything else she had ever seen. As she scattered it, Pirube said a blessing.

"Sweet spirits, watch over these souls. Keep them in a deep, beautiful sleep, free from worry until we return. Give them the sweetest dreams they have ever had and let them remember all of their beautiful dreams when they awake. Let the angels watch over them."

With that Bidu heard what sounded like angels singing. The room was filled with such beautiful music.

"Pirube, do you hear that?"

"Yes, Bidu, that is how we know the spell is cast because it is blessed by the angels and they are here now." Then she turned to Bidu. "It's time for us to go back to your room. We have more to do before we can leave."

Bidu could feel her heart beating. She was so excited. As soon as they got back to her room, she asked,

"Now what, Pirube?"

"You will need to lie flat on the floor so I can reach all of you to sprinkle the fairy dust. You must lie still, be very quiet, and just listen to my words. All the while I am casting the spell, you must feel as much love in your heart as you can. You must know with no doubt that you will be safe. Once you are in that state, and the fairy dust is all sprinkled, you will become a fairy just like me. Are you ready?"

"Yes, oh yes!" cried Bidu. She laid down on the floor just like Pirube told her to do.

"Now close your eyes and just feel the love."

Bidu closed her eyes. She thought she could feel the fairy dust lightly falling on her skin as she listened to Pirube cast the spell.

"Sweet spirits, cover Bidu in my fairy dust, like a blanket of love. Let her feel safe and protected. Let her learn all the ways of the fairies. Give her the powers of healing and sharing so that she can know the greatest joy of being a fairy. Let us be fairy sisters in this world and beyond. Forevermore."

Again, they heard the angels. Then it was quiet for a minute.

"Bidu, you can open your eyes now."

Bidu slowly opened her eyes. She looked just like Pirube! She was so small, but she still felt like herself. Her heart felt so full. She couldn't remember ever feeling this happy.

"Let's try your wings," said Pirube.

"How do I do that?" asked Bidu.

"They are on your back. Think about them. Think that they are fluttering. See them fluttering, and they will."

Bidu tried and tried, but nothing happened.

"You have to trust, Bidu. You must believe!" Pirube told her. "You see, you are a real fairy now, so BE one."

Bidu dug down deep in her soul. "I'm a fairy and I can fly. I'm a fairy and I can fly. I'm a fairy and I can fly." And with that, her wings began to flutter, just a little at first. Soon she could feel herself lifting off the ground.

"Oh my," she sang out, "I can fly! I can fly! Come fly with me, Pirube." But as soon as she said that, she remembered that Pirube's wing was hurt.

"Pirube, please tell me how to fix your wing. I want to heal you."

Pirube just smiled.

"Why didn't you say something?" Bidu asked.

"I had to wait for you to offer it," Pirube answered. "I can't ask for it for myself because the healing wouldn't work that way. But now that you have offered, I can help you to help me."

"What should I do?" asked Bidu.

"You must make some fairy dust of your own. Move your arms like this." She moved her arms in the same circular motion as when she put the spell on Bidu's parents. It took a few tries but, all of a sudden, Bidu was covered in beautiful fairy dust.

"What do I do now?" she asked Pirube.

"You are a real fairy now. You have all the powers of a real fairy. Just spread the fairy dust on my wing, and the words of the healing will come to you. I can't tell you what to say, or it won't work."

Bidu gently took the wrapping off Pirube's wing. Then she sprinkled fairy dust all over it, and just like Pirube said, the words came spilling out.

"Sweet spirits, surround Pirube's wing in this fairy dust. Heal her wing so that it is like brand new. Let her fly again to be with her family. Restore all her powers to find her way and make her whole again. Protect her as we make our journey."

Then Bidu was quiet. So was Pirube. They both waited. Soon, the angels sang. Bidu could see Pirube's wing starting to flutter, slowly at first, then faster and faster.

"Oh Bidu, you did it! You are a true fairy and now you are my fairy sister. You have healed me!" Pirube gave Bidu a long, beautiful hug. They couldn't do that when Bidu was girl size.

They hugged and laughed and cried together. Then Pirube moved away.

"I could hug you forever and we will hug a lot more, but now, we need to go. Open the window just enough for us to get out. This is the way we will also return. You have your own direction finders, but it will be easier if you just stay close to me for your first flight. I can't wait to show you my land and all the ways of the fairies."

And with that, Pirube took Bidu's hand as they took off together into the night.

3

The Fairy Hunters

"Stay with me," Pirube told Bidu. "We have to stay away from the lights. We don't want to be spotted."

Bidu wondered if she should be afraid. "Why don't we want to be spotted, Pirube? Is there something I should know?"

Pirube answered. "There are actually fairy hunters out there, but they only come out at night because they can only see us in the lights at night."

"Why only at night?" Bidu asked.

"During the day we have sunlight which doesn't light us up, but if we get into the lights at night, then we light up like crazy because the night lights reflect off our wings. That's why we will want to stay in the dark."

"Oh," said Bidu as her heart started to beat faster. "But I can't see as well in the pitch black of the night." She didn't want to feel afraid, but she did.

"Don't worry, Bidu. Just stay with me. We have our wings and we can navigate perfectly, it's just that…"

"Just that what?" interrupted Bidu. "Just that what?"

"Stop flying for a moment. I need to talk to you," said Pirube.

She landed on a lily pad that was floating in the lake by Bidu's house. Bidu landed right next to her.

"Bidu, I need to tell you some things that I haven't told you yet."

"What?" asked Bidu with concern.

Pirube went on. "As a fairy, you have to take certain precautions. There are some bad people out there who want to capture us. They want our fairy dust and our magic, but they don't really want us. Do you know what I mean?"

Bidu thought that even Pirube seemed a little afraid. "I think so," said Bidu.

Pirube continued. "Just stay close to me. We will stay away from any night lights. I will make it so that when we speak, only we can hear each other and no one else can hear us until we get to my land. We don't want the fairy hunters to have any idea that we might be here. I'm so glad you are with me because it makes me feel safer."

"I'm happy I can be with you," said Bidu. "But why don't we just wait until tomorrow and go in the daylight?"

"It's better for your parents for us to go now so that it will just be like a normal night for them. I'm sure that it will all work out, so please believe me."

"It's OK, Pirube. I'm here with you and for you. It will all be OK. Soon we'll be back to your home."

"You always make me feel better," Pirube said softly. "I'm so glad you found me and I love that we are fairy sisters. Now be still for a minute so I can silence our voices to everyone but each other. All you have to do is know and believe."

Pirube waved her arms again, just like she did when she put the spell on Bidu's parents. Bidu sat quietly while the spell was cast.

"OK, let's try it out. See that bird over there?"

"Yes," said Bidu. "I see it."

"Let's fly over and yell as loud as we can. If the bird doesn't fly away, then it's working. Let's go."

They flew together a short way to where the bird was peacefully sitting on his own lily pad.

"OK," said Pirube. "Start yelling!"

"HEYYYYY!" they both yelled, but the bird just sat still.

"Great," said Pirube. "Now we need to go. We don't want to fly too high because the currents are too fast up high. Just stay with me."

"I will be right here," Bidu reassured Pirube. Even though Bidu was a little scared, she didn't want to make Pirube afraid, so she tried to stay strong for her.

Pirube took off again, but looked back to make sure that Bidu was right there and she was.

They flew for a while. Bidu started to relax and enjoy flying with her new fairy wings. She stayed as close to Pirube as she could, but Pirube could fly much faster than her. Bidu kept trying to keep up so she could stay close. They were about 15 feet apart when, all of a sudden, so many lights came on. They were floodlights and the sky lit up like crazy.

Pirube yelled at Bidu. "It's the fairy hunters lighting up the sky. Go down low… to the ground."

Bidu didn't stop for a minute. She headed straight to the ground to get out of the lights. Since Pirube was higher up, she couldn't get there as fast. Then Bidu heard Pirube again.

"Keep going, Bidu. I've been caught in a net and I can't get out. Save yourself."

Bidu didn't know what to do. She wanted to go back to Pirube, but she didn't want to be caught too.

"Hold on, Pirube. I will find a way to save you." Bidu was hoping that the silent spell was working so that she could keep talking to her fairy sister. She found a little hole in the ground and she hid in it. She was shaking.

From the hole she was hiding in, she could see what was happening up above. The fairy hunters were all shouting.

"We got one! We got one! Let's take her back to our camp and get her fairy dust."

They must not have seen Bidu, because they never said anything about another fairy.

Bidu knew she had to stay low and out of the lights but she also had to stay close to Pirube so that she didn't lose her. She wished she could fly home to get her daddy to help her, but he was under the spell that Pirube had put on him and he wouldn't recognize her anyway. She was scared and alone, but she wouldn't leave Pirube. Somehow, she would find a way to save her.

The hunters turned off the big floodlights, but they still had flashlights so they could see how to get back to their camp. Bidu knew she would have to stay behind them so their flashlights would be in front of her. That way they wouldn't be able to see her, but she could still stay close to them. After all, she was very small now and they might not notice because they were busy celebrating the capture of a real fairy.

They were all shouting and laughing. "We got one!"

"I wonder what the fairy dust will be worth?"

"Yeah, we'll all be rich!"

"Let's see if we can get her magic powers."

Then the big boss said, "Stop talking. Let's get her back to camp. Pack everything up."

Bidu was feeling sicker by the minute. How could they talk about Pirube that way? How could they not see how delicate and fragile she was? How could they only think of themselves and their own selfish wants? Bidu was determined to save Pirube. She wanted to make them regret what they had done.

She knew that Pirube couldn't see her where she was. She wanted to reassure her that she was close by. She could only hope that Pirube could FEEL her nearby.

Meanwhile, Pirube was frozen in the net. She couldn't move. She was so scared, but still she was worried about Bidu. She hoped that Bidu was able to escape. She wanted to struggle, but she was so tight in the net that she couldn't move. Not even a little bit. She had heard stories about the fairy hunters and how they wanted to get the fairy dust. She didn't know what was going to happen, but she was afraid. She decided it was best to just lie still because she didn't want to hurt her wing again. Then she called out to Bidu.

"Bidu, are you near?"

"Yes, Pirube, I'm right behind you. I'm trying to stay out of the light."

"I have an idea," shouted Pirube. "You are a fairy now. That means you have all the powers and magic of a fairy as long as you only use it for good. I can't put a spell on anything because I can't make fairy dust right now and I can't move my arms to make dust or a spell."

"Oh, Pirube," said Bidu. "What should I do? I don't know how to make a spell."

"Yes, you do, Bidu. You made a spell to heal my wing, remember? You can do this. I want you to make yourself invisible."

"What if something goes wrong? I won't know how to make it back."

Pirube could hear in Bidu's voice that she was scared.

"I know it's scary when you're first trying to cast spells, but I know you and I'm telling you that you can do it. I will tell you exactly how."

Bidu knew that she had healed Pirube's wing, but somehow that didn't feel like a 'real' spell to her. She knew she had seen Pirube do it, but mostly her eyes were closed during those spells. She knew she had to listen carefully. She just had to try.

"OK, Pirube, tell me exactly what to do and I will do it."

Pirube thought for a minute. She didn't want to leave anything out.

"Bidu, first calm yourself. Take a deep breath. It's like when you healed my wing and the words just came to you. When you make a spell, you will have to say exactly what you want in the spell. Ask to be invisible to everyone except me. Ask this for me because it will help me. You can't ask for something just for yourself, remember? While you are asking, you must move your arms in a clockwise motion. You have to move them exactly the same way at the same time. Most importantly, you must believe."

"Why don't I make you invisible too?" asked Bidu.

"Because fairies can only make themselves invisible if it's to help another. I would have to make myself invisible, but I'm so tight in this net that I can't move. Oh, Bidu, I'm scared."

Bidu felt butterflies in her stomach, but she knew she had to do this. She dug down to muster up all the courage she could find. She thought only of Pirube and helping her. She moved her arms just the way she'd seen Pirube do it. Then she spoke.

"Sweet spirits, make me invisible so that only Pirube can see me. I ask this so that I can help her. Help me to know and do all the right things to get her back to her land. Let the angels watch over her and protect her."

It was silent for a moment. Then Bidu could hear the angels just like when Pirube put the sleeping spell on her parents.

"I think it worked because I hear the angels. Pirube, do you hear them?"

"Yes, Bidu. You are a wonderful fairy. Now you can be right with me while we talk. We need to make a plan while they can't hear us. I haven't been paying close attention. I have no idea where they have taken us. This net is hurting me. I need to get out." Pirube started to cry.

Just then, they both heard the boss hunter giving orders.

"Take her into the tent and hang her in the net on the pole."

It hurt Bidu to see what they were doing to Pirube. How could she get her free?

"Just lie still, Pirube. Don't worry. I will figure something out."

One of the hunters took the net that was holding Pirube, tied it in a knot and hung it on the pole. He said, "Why don't we take her out of the net and get her fairy dust?"

Then the boss was yelling orders again. "We'll take her out when I say to take her out. I'm the boss here. I want her still, wrapped tight and scared so that when I tell her to do what I want, she will do it."

Bidu couldn't believe he could be so mean.

The boss went on. "Let's get some rest. She'll never get out of that net. Tomorrow she'll be willing to do anything we want. Now all of you get out. I will stay in the tent and guard her."

The boss made sure everyone was out of the tent. Once everyone was gone, he sat down. Bidu got a really good look at him. He looked as mean as he acted. He had a big belly, and a scary face. He looked like a pirate. He even had a bandana on his head.

He started to talk to Pirube.

"You are my fairy now. You will do everything I tell you to do or you will never get out of here. I'm going to take all of your powers and all of your fairy dust. After I get what I want, you will no longer be of value to me. Then, I will throw you away in the lake." He laughed the most awful and sinister laugh Bidu had ever heard. He took a big drink of something that smelled awful. He watched Pirube for a while until he fell asleep.

"Pirube, what do we do now? How can I release the net?"

Pirube was sounding weaker from being wrapped so tightly. "I can't tell you what to do for me, Bidu. Don't you remember that?"

Bidu felt her stomach drop. She didn't know what to do. She wished she had scissors and she told that to Pirube.

"Bidu," said Pirube. "Think like a fairy, and not like a little girl. Be quiet for a minute. Go inside yourself for an answer."

Bidu closed her eyes. She started praying to the angels. All of sudden, the answer popped into her head.

"Pirube?" she called out.

"Yes, Bidu."

"I'm not a little girl right now. I'm a real fairy. I am going to do something good for you. I need you to believe with me."

Bidu went over to Pirube in the net. She started to move her arms in the circular motion as she said these words:

"Sweet spirits, release Pirube from this bondage. Restore her energy and make her whole."

In an instant, the net was split open but Pirube didn't fall to the ground. She floated.

When she landed, she just laid there for a minute. Then she slowly tried to move her wings, then her arms and legs.

"Oh Bidu, you did it. Once again, I couldn't tell you what to do for me, but you figured it out. Your heart is so full of love that the spirits heard you. Now let's go home."

"Wait, Pirube, can you make yourself invisible now?" asked Bidu. "There are lights out there and I can still hear some of the hunters. They are not all asleep yet."

"Oh, I almost forgot. I'm so discombobulated."

Pirube started to move her arms and soon she was invisible just like Bidu. Her wings were sore, but she tried to flap them slowly at first to get them moving again. It took a while, but soon she was flying around in the tent.

"OK, Bidu," she said. "I think I'm ready to go."

Bidu thought a moment. "You know, Pirube, when I was watching these mean hunters and what they were doing to you, I wanted to hurt them. I wanted to make them regret what they did. I thought of some terrible punishments I could do to them. But then I just realized that I was thinking like they think. I don't want to be like that… ever! I would like to do one more spell. A fairy spell. Can I make it work on all of the hunters at the same time?"

"Yes, you can. You just need to be in their vicinity. We are close enough to make it work for all of them right where we are."

"OK then," Bidu said. She took a deep breath to relax. Even though the hunters wanted to capture fairies and take everything good they had, she wanted to wait until she had no bad thoughts about them while she was casting the spell.

After a few deep breaths, she was ready. She looked at Pirube.

"Do you want to know what I'm going to say?"

Pirube smiled. "I know your sweet heart. I believe you will say exactly the right words. I will hear it when you say it for real. Go ahead whenever you're ready."

Bidu took one more deep breath and then she began.

"Sweet spirits, soften the hearts of the hunters. Where there is hatred, fill that space with love. Where there is meanness, fill that space with kindness. Where there is greed, fill that space with generosity. Where there is selfishness, fill that space with thoughtfulness and compassion. Let them forget about ever hunting fairies again. From this day on, let them only want peace, tolerance and love for everyone. Let this spell start now and last forevermore."

Then came the sweet sounds of the angels.

"Oh, Bidu! That was beautiful!" said Pirube. "What a great gift you have given to them and to everyone they will ever meet in their lives. You, too, will be blessed always for your gesture of kindness. You are a true fairy! I'm so proud of you."

Bidu smiled. She did appreciate Pirube's words, but she didn't need to hear anything. It just felt good to cast that spell on those men. All she really wanted was to see the results of the spell.

"Do you think we will see any real change?" she asked Pirube.

"Well, since they can't hear us and they can't see us, why don't we step outside the tent and see what we can see."

They left the tent together and saw the hunters all around the fire, but they sounded so different. They were still talking.

"Hey, John, can I get you another cup of coffee?"

"Why, thank you, Mark. That's very sweet of you. Let me get the cups. In fact, why don't we serve coffee to everyone?"

"Great idea," said Mark.

"I think your spell worked very well." Pirube started giggling. Then Bidu started to giggle too.

Bidu mimicked Mark. "Hey Pirube, can I get you a cup of coffee?"

Then they both laughed until they cried. They were so happy.

"I think we should get going, Bidu. I so want to go home. And I want my family to meet you. Are you ready to go?"

"Oh yes, I'm so excited!" exclaimed Bidu. "Let's go."

"OK," replied Pirube. "But let's stay invisible and silent until we see my land... just to be safe. I think I've had enough adventure for one night."

"Me too," said Bidu.

Once again, the fairy sisters took flight, joined hands in the air and let their wings take them home. They held hands the entire way. They didn't need to speak a word. They were just happy to be together and to have escaped their ordeal.

After flying for about an hour, Pirube exclaimed, "Oh look! Over there!" She pointed to something.

Bidu couldn't see it yet, but she knew what Pirube was seeing.

They were coming into Fairyland.

4

Fairyland

Bidu was so excited to see that they were getting close to Pirube's home. She couldn't believe that soon she would be in a land of fairies. She always knew fairies were real, but she had never seen one until she met Pirube. Now, not only had she seen one, but she had become a fairy herself! This was so amazing to her. As they got closer, the sun was starting to rise. She could see the light from the sun as it shone on Pirube's homeland.

"Oh look, Pirube," Bidu said excitedly. "Is that it over there with all the amazing flowers?"

"Yes, Bidu," Pirube answered. "I knew you would know right away. I can't wait to show you my land and for everyone to meet you. They are going to love you just as I do."

"Oh, Pirube, I am so excited!" Bidu exclaimed.

"Hold my hand all the way," Pirube said. "I will guide you in for a smooth landing."

Bidu held tight to Pirube's hand as they began their descent down to the village. As they got closer, Bidu could see the little village and the small houses. It was just like a human town, only so much smaller. There were flowers everywhere and lots of birds and butterflies.

"Oh look!" cried Bidu. "Are those baby foxes over there?" She pointed down to her right.

"Yes, they are. Foxes are our guardians and safe keepers. They watch over us and help us. There are many in our land and this is the season for the babies to be born, so there will be lots of babies for you to see. And once you change back into a girl, you can hold them all."

Bidu couldn't believe it! Baby foxes were her favorite animal. She felt like she was in a dream.

"Bidu, I need you to do exactly as I say so you can have a smooth landing. Hold my hand, slow down your wing flapping, and we will glide in slowly and land on our feet. Do you see that big green grassy area?"

"Yes, I do," said Bidu.

"We will aim to land there. Slow your flapping. There you go. Now just hold your wings out and let the breeze take you in."

Bidu did exactly as Pirube said and they slowly floated down to the patch of grass. As they landed, there were several other fairies and foxes there to greet them.

"Piru, Piru (*like the country Peru*), is that you?" they called out. "Oh my, come look. It's Piru. She's back!"

Bidu couldn't help but ask. "I thought your name is Pirube. Why are they calling you Piru?"

Piru answered in her gentle voice. "My real name is Pirube. But my family calls me Piru. It's like a nickname. Only those closest to me call me Piru."

"I love that name," Bidu said. "And it rhymes with MY name."

Piru smiled. "Then please, call me Piru. It's like we are family now anyway. And I didn't notice that our names rhyme. That's great. Bidu and Piru. Perfect! From now on I am Piru, your fairy soul sister."

By then, all the fairies were surrounding them.

"Who is this? What land does she come from? She looks like us, but she's not from here. Did she hurt you? Are you OK, Piru?"

"Hold on, hold on," laughed Piru. "This is Bidu. She saved me and healed my hurt wing. She took me in and made me feel comfortable. She is good and sweet and I want you all to meet her. You will love her."

They all seemed so curious about this new fairy. Some of them came right up to her, and others stayed way back.

"Your parents have been so worried about you, Piru. You've never been gone so long."

"I know, Mali," said Piru. "I flew into a tree and hurt my wing and I couldn't fly. Bidu rescued me. Everyone, come close and meet Bidu. She is wonderful and kind and she helped me. It's OK to come close."

Bidu smiled. She so wanted them to like her. They were all so small, and so cute. For a moment she forgot she was small too. She wanted to pick them all up and hold them.

Piru spoke. "Let's go home. I want to see my parents." Piru took Bidu by the hand and said, "Come Bidu. I can't wait for you to meet my mother and father."

"OK, Piru," Bidu said as she held tight. She liked the name Piru. It sounded sweet and it felt wonderful to say.

They all started walking to the village. All the fairies were talking excitedly. "Piru is back. Come see. She's here."

More and more of the fairies were filling the streets. There were so many of them and they all seemed so happy.

"Only one more street until my street," Piru told Bidu. "We're almost there."

Finally, they reached a little fairy cottage. It was cream colored and the windows were trimmed with a beautiful light pink. There were pink and white flowers in the garden. Bidu could see two fairies coming out of the house. When they saw Piru, her mother started to cry.

"Oh Piru, I was so scared. I didn't know where you were or if I would ever see you again." She grabbed Piru and held her for a long time. Then her father gave her a long hug too.

"Oh, honey," he said. "I missed you so much."

Then they noticed Bidu.

"And who is this?" her father asked.

"This is my new friend. She saved me. Her name is Bidu."

"Well, hello Bidu," said Piru's mother. "Thank you for helping our little girl. Please come into our home. You must be so tired."

Bidu felt very welcomed. Piru's parents were so nice and so loving.

As they walked into the cottage, Bidu noticed all of the small furnishings. Inside by the fire, there was a mother fox and her three babies.

"Oh, look at the baby foxes. They are my favorite animal!" exclaimed Bidu. "But we don't usually have them for pets in human world. They are in the wild."

"In human world?" asked her mother. "What do you know of the human world?"

"Mama," interrupted Piru. "I have something to tell you and Daddy. Bidu is really a human girl. I would never have survived if she hadn't found me and rescued me. She helped heal my wing and she is my true friend. I thought it might be scary for you all to meet her as a girl because she's so much bigger than us, so I changed her into one of us." Piru looked at Bidu and they both started to giggle.

Her father had something to say. "Piru's mother and I thank you for helping our daughter, Bidu. My name is Dartu (*Dar-too*), and Piru's mother is called Lila (*Lie-la*). We are happy to meet you and have you in our home. We will treat you as family now and we will share stories of our land with you and you can share stories of your land with us."

"I want to hear all about your village and how the foxes became such a big part of it," said Bidu.

"Foxes are very important here in our village," said Dartu. "Did Piru tell you?"

"Not really," said Bidu.

Dartu took a deep breath. "Let's go sit by the fire and I will tell you an amazing story about the foxes in our land."

They all got cozy by the fire, and Dartu began his story.

"Many years ago, we shared this land with the black-footed demons. They were mean and wicked and they wanted to own and control all the land. They didn't want to share it with anyone else. At that time there were also the fairies, the foxes, the mildrites, and the dwarfs. Everyone had their own village in the land and stayed within their own village. The fairies got along with everyone. But the black-footed demons didn't get along with anyone. They always wanted to go to war to take control of all the land. The mildrites had the biggest part of the land but they were peaceful. They tried to talk with the demons to work out a peaceful treaty so that everyone could live without war. The demons lied to the mildrites and fooled them into believing they wanted peace. Then one day, when they weren't prepared for war, the demons attacked them. They captured most of the mildrites and put them all in jail. Then they turned them into servants and slaves and took over their village. The dwarfs were worried because they were the next closest village and they were all small. The demons were like giants. The dwarfs didn't think they could protect their village, so they too tried to talk to the demons. The demons said that if the dwarfs did not give up their village by the next Friday at noon, they would come in and take it. Then the dwarfs could become their servants and slaves just like the mildrites. The dwarfs were frantic. They knew that the fairies wanted to stay out of any fighting but the dwarfs didn't know where else to turn.

They came to the high council of the fairies to plead for their help.

'Please, help us,' said Balor (*Bay-lor*), the ruler of the dwarfs.

'Whatever could we do?' said Arion, the prince of the fairies. 'We are even smaller than you are.'

'Yes,' replied Balor, 'but you have magic powers.'

Arion tried to explain that fairy powers are only to be used to help others, not to hurt anyone.

'There must be a way,' replied Balor.

With that, the prince thought for a moment and then said, 'Why don't we ask the foxes to join us. Perhaps we can all work together.'

Balor laughed. 'Foxes are animals. They can't think like we can. What could they possibly do?'

'We'll never know, if we don't ask,' said Arion.

That afternoon he went to the leader of the foxes to arrange for a meeting to take place the next day. The foxes agreed and seemed happy to be invited.

The next day, the sun came up and settled in a clear blue sky. All of the attendees were looking forward to meeting. They had decided it would be best to meet in the furthest land away from the demons – the village of the foxes. The prince went with high hopes and a positive attitude although he didn't know what to expect. The dwarfs were hopeful, but they couldn't see how animals could help. As they sat down for their meeting, Balor was shocked to hear the fox speak. He said, 'My name is Koda. I am glad that you want to meet with us. We want to live in harmony, but the demons make it impossible. We want to help.'

Balor could not believe his ears. 'Please, go on,' he said to the fox. 'What can we do?'

'Well,' said Koda. 'It seems to me that the dwarf village is the next most in danger. We can't possibly compete with the giant demons. They can crush us. We have to outsmart them. We can't use fairy magic unless we can figure out how to use it for good. Both the dwarfs and the fairies just can't think viciously like the demons. But we foxes are sly. We are clever. And no one expects us to be smart, but we are. If we can take all the best parts of each village, we should be able to defeat the demons.'

The fairy prince was so happy. 'Let's come up with a plan that will do just what you suggest.'

Then Balor blurted out, 'We can't have peace until we kill all the demons.'

Koda looked deep into the eyes of the dwarf. 'You are a peaceful people. The fairies are peaceful and loving. I said we need to outsmart them, not kill them.'

The dwarf ruler was upset. 'They will never let us live in peace and we will always live in fear.'

The prince agreed with Koda. 'We must do what is in our nature and our nature is to do good. I just can't figure out how exactly to do this. We have no plan and we are not prepared.'

Balor reminded them that they only had until Friday at noon. Koda spoke softly, but with great authority. 'Let us go now and meet with the fox elders. They will know what to do. We will have a plan by tonight.'"

Bidu was on the edge of her seat, listening to every word of Dartu's story. She couldn't wait to hear how the demons were defeated so that they could all live in peace, but she also never wanted the story to end. Piru smiled. She knew what was coming and she also couldn't wait for Bidu to hear the whole story.

Dartu continued. "Balor, Arion and Koda sat down with the fox elders. Koda told the elders all that was going on. They knew how wicked the demons were and how they had taken over the mildrites. They wanted to save all the villages in the land and even free the mildrites if they could. They all agreed they wanted to do it as peacefully as possible. Balor still wasn't sure this was such a good idea. He was very afraid for his village of dwarfs, but still he listened to every word once the chief elder began to speak.

'We must come up with a plan so we can be victorious. We must utilize the best parts of each village.'

'What are the best parts of each village?' asked Balor.

The elder continued. 'We must use the dwarfs as our best warriors, the foxes for their cleverness, and the fairies for their magic.'

Balor interrupted. 'But we don't want to fight. We are not warriors. That's a bad plan.'

Arion could see that Balor was very nervous and afraid. Koda tried to calm him. 'Balor, you must be certain that we can work together. There is nothing to be afraid of. Perhaps warrior is not the right word. Wait until you hear the entire plan. We all must KNOW that we will find a way. Please try to be calm and listen to the elder.'

Balor bowed his head and then spoke. 'OK, I know you are right. I will try to stay calm.'

Koda went over to Balor and gently put his head in Balor's lap. Balor stroked the fox and was ready to listen. The elder began to lay out the plan.

'The demons are fighters. They want to fight. We must let them think they are coming into Dwarfland for that fight. When they went to capture the mildrites, they all went. Not one demon stayed back. This will happen again, but we will be ready.'

Balor again interrupted. 'But we don't want to battle. We can't possibly beat them.'

'Balor, please wait,' Arion said. 'We haven't heard the entire plan yet.'

Balor got quiet and let the elder continue. 'Let's talk about the foxes for a minute. Foxes are very good at burrowing tunnels and digging holes in the ground. There is a very large field in the middle of Dwarfland. We will burrow it all under the ground. We will go very deep but from the top it will just look like the same big field... perfect for the battle that the demons are looking to have. The dwarfs will prepare as though they will go into battle as well. It must look real. They will stand on the far side of the field so that the demons have to walk across to get to them.'

The elder could see that Balor was getting ready to interrupt again.

'Balor,' said the elder. 'You must have faith. Go back to your people and prepare them for battle. Build cannons and make armor so that when the demons see you all standing ready, they will think they will get their battle. They will rush at you all at once, but I promise you there really won't be a battle.'

'How can that be?' Balor asked.

The elder spoke again. 'The foxes will have prepared the ground under the field.'

'What do you mean, you will have prepared the ground?' Balor asked.

The elder smiled and tried to reassure Balor. 'Once all of the demons are on the field, the enormous weight of them all will cause the field to collapse. The foxes will have burrowed it so that it will be very weak and, once it collapses, then all of the demons will be at the bottom of the huge hole in the ground. Since it will be so deep, they will not be able to climb out.'

'Then they will all die?' asked Balor.

'NO!' shouted Koda. 'I told you, no killing.'

'Well, whatever will we do with all the demons?' Balor asked.

Arion had a question too. 'What part will the fairies play? We don't go to war and we can't dig holes.'

The elder continued. 'The fairies will do what they do best. They will be ready to cast a spell of goodness on all of the demons for the good of our land. And then we will free all the mildrites, or better yet, the demons will free them.'

The room was quiet. Everyone was thinking about this plan and if it could really work. Alone, the fairies couldn't do it. Alone, the dwarfs couldn't do it. Alone, the foxes couldn't do it. But together... together, maybe, just maybe they could do it. They had to try. It was their only hope or the demons would eventually take over all the villages.

'Now,' said the elder. 'Are there any more questions?'

The room was quiet. They all looked at each other. No one seemed to know what to say, but they all knew they had to try. 'It is a good plan and I believe we can carry it out, with all of us together. Are we in agreement?'

Arion nodded his head.

Koda nodded his head.

Balor had his head bowed down. He slowly picked up his head and looked at each of the other leaders. Then he too, nodded.

The elder spoke. 'Very good. Now go to your lands and prepare. We will be ready when they come on Friday. May the spirits guide and direct us, watch over and protect us. We need not be afraid. The plan is now in motion...'"

Dartu paused. Bidu couldn't be quiet. "What happened? Did they battle? Did the plan work?"

Piru giggled. Dartu and Lila laughed too. Dartu said, "Maybe I'll wait until tomorrow to finish the story."

"Oh no!" cried Bidu. "I can't wait! It's so exciting!"

"OK, Bidu," said Dartu as he winked at Piru. "Where was I?"

"The plan is now in motion," said Bidu.

"Oh yes… the battle." Dartu took a deep breath and continued...

5

The Battle

Bidu was listening to every word. Her eyes were so big with excitement as she heard Dartu tell of the battle:

"Arion, Koda, and Balor left the meeting together. Once they were out of earshot, Balor blurted out, 'Do you really think this can work? I'm so afraid the demons will get our land.'

Koda spoke first. 'Balor, you must have faith. You must not show this fear to the other dwarfs or you will make them afraid. You have to be strong for them so they feel secure that this plan will work. You must show them confidence and strength.'

Balor shook his head. 'I know, I know, but I've never done battle before. I don't know anything about building cannons or making armor. None of us do.'

Koda nuzzled Balor's arm. 'You must not worry. The cannons don't need to fire. The battle won't get that far. And the armor will be material that you sew together to look like armor.'

Arion thought for a moment. 'I think the fairies might be able to help with the armor.'

'Really? How?' asked Balor.

'Well,' said Arion, 'we make fairy dust. Fairy dust sparkles so bright, like gold and silver all mixed together. It glows and shines the brightest in the sunlight. If the sun shines right on it, it can almost be blinding. At noon, when they come, the sun will be directly overhead. That will put us in the perfect position so that when the sun shines down on our costumes, it will look just like shiny metal armor.'

Balor was listening intently. 'I think I understand.'

He looked a little more confident now.

'So, we can just sew a costume that looks like armor and then if you sprinkle us with fairy dust, it will look like the real thing?'

'Yes,' answered Arion. 'Exactly! And since all you dwarfs make your own clothes, I know you all know how to sew! Think of it like you are just making costumes!'

Balor was smiling now. He understood, and for the first time he actually thought this plan could work.

Koda could see that Balor was feeling much better, so he decided it was time for him to go.

'Balor,' he said, 'I trust that you will go now and talk to all the dwarfs and get going on your costumes. I must hurry to tell the foxes about our plan. They have lots of burrowing to do and not a lot of time to do it. Let us all meet on Wednesday to see where we are in the process.'

'Yes,' said Arion. 'I need to get back to Fairyland because it will take us all working nonstop to make enough fairy dust by Friday.'

The leaders all looked at each other. They all nodded and knew what they had to do.

'We will meet here again on Wednesday at noon to see how we are progressing,' said Koda.

With that, they all went in separate directions. Arion turned left to go to Fairyland, Balor turned right to go to Dwarfland, and Koda headed straight to Foxland. After a few steps, they all turned around one last time to wish good luck to each other. They now knew the plan and how to make it happen.

As Balor approached Dwarfland, he was greeted by all of the dwarfs. They were waiting to see what had taken place because they felt so threatened by the demons. Balor had a new stronger attitude and he was confident as he told the dwarfs what they needed to do.

'We need to get busy sewing our battle costumes. The fairies will cover us in fairy dust and it will look like we are all wearing shiny armor.'

He was interrupted by his brother, Garton. 'And then what are we supposed to do? Is this going to be dangerous? Are we going to try to fight the demons?'

Balor could see that Garton was nervous just like he had been at first. He understood Garton's apprehension. He tried to reassure him just the way Koda and Arion had reassured him at the beginning.

'We have a very good plan. For now let's just get busy making our costumes. On Wednesday, I will meet with Koda and Arion again, and then we will tell all of you exactly what needs to be done. We will win, so let's try not to worry right now. We need to be focused on what we have to do.'

Garton had a look of deep concern on his face, but he trusted his older brother.

'OK, Balor,' he said. 'I will get started.'

'Remember,' said Balor. 'We will be covered in fairy dust, so use whatever fabric you can find. The color doesn't matter. Now go to tell everyone what needs to be done and have them get busy!'

'OK,' said Garton. 'I've got it!'

Within an hour all of the dwarfs were sewing. It was amazing to see how they all worked together.

****

Arion arrived at Fairyland to be greeted by the fairies. They were so happy he was back, and they couldn't wait to hear the plan. They had been concerned they might not be able to help because they were so small. But as Arion got closer, they could see he was smiling, so they all felt that there might be some good news to hear.

'Fairy brothers and sisters,' Arion began. 'Gather around. I have good news. We will be able to help in a huge way and we will only have to do what we do best... make fairy dust. Lots and lots of fairy dust.'

'Why do we need to make so much?' asked one of the fairies.

Arion explained the plan to them and how they would need enough fairy dust to cover all of the dwarfs, and then a lot more after that.

'Why do we need a lot more?'

Arion didn't want to tell them everything just yet. He thought it best for them to get to work making all they would need to cover the dwarfs' costumes, and then after the meeting on Wednesday, he would tell them about the rest of the plan. The fairies were very sensitive, and they needed to be calm to make good fairy dust. If they knew about the foxes burrowing, and the demons falling into a pit, Arion was concerned that it might disrupt the peace they needed to make as much fairy dust as was required.

'Let's not get ahead of ourselves,' said Arion. 'Let's just get to work making as much fairy dust as we can. As always, let's make it with love and goodness, so that it works for whatever good we do.'

Most of the fairies knew that Arion would tell them all they needed to know, so they accepted what he said and they happily got to work. Arion was busy calculating just how much fairy dust was needed. He was secretly a little worried about making so much in such a short time, but he didn't let the other fairies see his concern. He wanted them to work and be happy because making fairy dust is always such a joy for a fairy and he wanted them all to feel as much joy as possible.

****

Koda approached Foxland. All of the foxes were there, ready and willing to do whatever was necessary. They were so happy that the dwarfs had called on them to help. This was the first time they were all working on something together. Koda knew how important the contribution of the foxes was going to be. Even though the foxes and the dwarfs and the fairies didn't fight, they really hadn't had much to do with each other before this. Koda was happy that they were all talking to each other and helping each other. It felt so good! He was happy to share all the information with the other foxes. 'We have a very important assignment. We will be helping to save Dwarfland. The fairies will be helping too so that we can defeat the demons and keep our land safe. This cannot be done without our participation.'

'What will we be doing?' they all cried out. 'Please tell us.'

They were all talking and asking questions.

'Hold on,' said Koda. 'I will tell you, but I can't talk when all of you are talking too.'

The excited foxes calmed down long enough for Koda to tell them the plan.

'You will all be doing what we do best. There is a very big field in Dwarfland. We need to burrow it so that the burrows are underground and hidden. All of our burrows will weaken the ground. This means we will only be able to make a few holes on the top of the ground at the sides of the field. Then when a lot of weight is put on the field, it will collapse. Since we are very light in weight and the demons are big and heavy, we will be safe while burrowing, but the land will collapse easily once the weight of the demons is upon it. The trick is that it can't collapse too quickly with just a little weight. We will have to make it so that it will hold up until all the demons are on the field and then, all at once, it will collapse. And the hole it makes must be big enough to hold all of the demons. We will have to plan very carefully where to start and end each tunnel.'

'What will we do with all the demons in a big hole?' asked one of the foxes.

'Don't worry about that,' Koda answered. 'We have a plan for that too. I will be meeting with the leaders from the dwarfs and the fairies on Wednesday and then you will know everything. For now, let us go to the field in Dwarfland so we can make our plans and begin burrowing.'

The foxes were so excited to be helping. They were always the lowest land in the kingdom. They were so happy for an opportunity to be a bigger part of the kingdom. They wanted to get started right away.

Koda led the way as they headed for the big field. The plan was now in motion."

****

Dartu paused as his eyes filled with tears.

"What's wrong?" asked Bidu, as she felt her eyes filling with tears too.

Dartu tried to compose himself. "Bidu, I'm touched by this story, because it's our history. It's real and true. And the fairies might not exist today if this battle had not occurred. My great grandparents actually lived through it. They were the fairies making all that fairy dust. I always feel emotionally touched when I think of how hard they must have worked for the success of the entire kingdom. All the while, they put all of their joy into that dust that saved the kingdom."

Bidu felt so much empathy for Dartu. She realized that this was not just a story he was telling, but that it really happened.

"Oh, Dartu, I can only imagine what that must have been like for your great grandparents."

Dartu smiled at Bidu. "I believe you feel it too, Bidu. But please don't feel bad. We are here now because of that battle. So it's all good. Would you like to hear how the battle was actually won?"

"Oh, yes!" cried Bidu. "I really would like to hear it all."

Dartu gave Bidu a look of love as he continued.

"Well," he began, "the dwarfs worked hard for several days sewing their costumes of armor. The fairies made fairy dust day and night to be sure they would have enough. The foxes were busy on the big field in Dwarfland burrowing tunnels. They had to be careful because if they got too close to each other and made the burrows too close, then the entire field could collapse before the demons ever got there.

Koda had every detail planned as to how to build the tunnels to be sure they were engineered perfectly for success. The foxes truly wanted to be of service so they followed his every detail. They had two teams. One team worked all day and the other team worked all night. By Wednesday, when Koda had to meet with the other leaders, they were almost finished. However, they still had to do the deepest part of the field and that was the most dangerous. The foxes were tired, but they would not give up. Koda told them all to rest on Wednesday so that they would have lots of energy for the bottom of the field. He thought they could finish it in one more day. He went back to the field on Wednesday morning to check all of the tunnels and make sure his plans were correct. He measured and measured to be sure he had it right so that the field would not collapse until all of the demons were on it. He was satisfied with his measurements and then it was time to meet with Balor and Arion.

All of the leaders had good reports. Arion said the fairies had made enough fairy dust for all of the dwarfs.

Koda asked, 'Do they have the fairy dust we need to put the spell on the demons?'

Arion paused. 'All the fairies are so tired. They have put everything into the fairy dust for the costumes.'

'How long do you think they need to make enough for when the demons are in the pit?' asked Koda.

'I think they can do it in one day, but they need to rest a bit.'

'I understand,' said Koda. 'And Balor, how are the dwarfs coming along with their costumes of armor?'

Balor answered, 'We have finished all of the costumes, but we still have to make helmets, if you think we need them.'

'How long will it take you to make the helmets?' asked Koda.

Balor thought for a moment. 'I think we can do it in one day. And we still need to make two cannons.'

Koda sat for a moment and then he spoke. 'We have all been working very hard. We have made great progress. Let's not work today anymore. Let everyone rest and relax. Tomorrow, the fairies will finish the fairy dust, the foxes will burrow the lower part of the field, and the dwarfs will make their helmets and cannons. Let us finish by tomorrow night, and then we will rest on Friday morning so that we can be ready when the demons come at noon.'

Balor and Arion agreed with this plan.

'Now,' Koda continued. 'Let's talk about how this will play out on Friday. Balor, you will need to have the dwarfs all in place on the south side of the field one hour before noon. You will have to line up by the markers that the foxes will set for you. They will set the markers Friday morning. We have checked the sun and the markers will be where the sun will shine the brightest at noon. Arion, you will need to be here with the fairy dust one hour before the demons are coming to coat all of the dwarfs with the dust. Will you be able to put the fairy dust on all of the dwarfs at that time?'

'Oh yes,' said Arion. 'We can spread the fairy dust very quickly. Every fairy will be there.'

'OK then,' Koda said. 'The foxes will finish burrowing the field tomorrow. We will all meet here one hour before noon on Friday. Agreed?'

Balor couldn't keep quiet. 'What if they come early and we're not prepared?'

Koda actually almost laughed. 'OK, Balor. You might have a point. Let's all meet three hours before noon to be sure. Is that better?'

Balor and Arion agreed that would be better. They would rather wait for the demons than be caught off guard. They all knew what they had to do. Friday would be here before they knew it.

Arion had a question too. 'Once all the demons are in the hole and the spell has been cast, how in the world will they ever get out of the hole? None of us are big enough to help them.'

Koda replied. 'Don't worry. I will have the foxes dig one large tunnel off to the side at the bottom of the hole with a stairway to the top. The demons won't be able to see it unless we tell them where it is and we won't tell them until we know it is safe.'

'Oh, Koda!' cried Balor. 'You have thought of everything. We couldn't do this without you.'

'The truth is, Balor, that we couldn't do it without each other. Now, let's get back to our lands and finish what we have started.'

They all agreed and went to get ready for a very big day of work.

On Thursday the fairies awoke at sunrise and began to make buckets and buckets of fairy dust. They had never made so much in one day, but they knew they needed enough to cover all the demons in the hole. The dwarfs were very busy making helmets and cannons. Each dwarf made their own helmet so they easily got them all done. Then they worked together to make two very real looking cannons.

The foxes had to work slowly and carefully to be sure the burrows would hold up just long enough for the demons to get on the field, and then it had to collapse all at once. It was quite an engineering feat and they all worked with such pride. Koda made one run through once they were done to check out all the tunnels and they were exactly as he designed them to be. There had been a few close calls, but in the end, the tunnels were perfect and the field was ready.

On Friday morning the sun came up and made a beautiful sunrise. There was not a cloud in the sky. It was going to be a sunny bright day, exactly what was needed for the fairy dust to shine. At nine o'clock, the dwarfs came marching in their costumes of armor.

They were in all colors because they'd had to use all of the fabric they had in their land to make enough costumes for everyone.

They met Koda as he arrived and they were directed to where they needed to line up. They were very careful not to set foot on the area where the tunnels had been dug out. Arion led the fairies and once the dwarfs were lined up, the fairies began to coat them in fairy dust. With the sun shining, it was so bright, it was almost impossible to look at for very long. Meanwhile, the foxes were standing guard watching for the demons who were supposed to come at noon, but at eleven o'clock, one hour before noon, the foxes cried out as they saw the demons coming to the field.

'The demons are coming! The demons are coming! They are coming right now! Hurry and get ready!'

Luckily, the fairies and the dwarfs were ready early. The dwarfs were already lined up covered in fairy dust.

Balor shouted, 'Are we all in our right places?'

Koda answered, 'Yes, Balor.'

'Does the armor look good?' asked Balor.

'Oh yes! The sun is shining perfectly on the armor. It's exactly what we wanted... even better!'

Balor seemed very happy. He smiled at Koda and Koda smiled back.

The fairies took their places in the big trees so that they would be safe and close by to spread all the rest of the fairy dust once the field turned into a big hole. Everyone could feel the ground shaking as the demons marched closer. When they spotted the dwarfs all standing across the field in their armor, they stopped. Their leader yelled out, 'CHARGE!' and all at once they started running toward the dwarfs. The dwarfs just stood still as they were supposed to do.

It didn't take very long for all of the demons to rush onto the field. They came closer and closer toward the dwarfs, but the dwarfs didn't move.

All of a sudden, the field rumbled like an earthquake and, in an instant, the field became a huge canyon. All of the demons were surprised and yelling and screaming. They didn't know what to do. It was like the ground opened up and swallowed them. They were thrashing around but there was no way out. The burrows were perfectly made and there was no possibility of anyone escaping. Once the demons knew they had been fooled, they were very angry and they were all shouting.

'We will get you for this!'

'Just wait until we get out of here!'

'We will take all of your lands and you will be our servants!'

Arion had to work fast. He called on the fairies to fly over the big hole and spread their fairy dust while he cast the spell.

'Sweet spirits, let this fairy dust change every heart. Even if only one speck of fairy dust touches any of the demons, let it surround each one of them in a blanket of love and kindness. Let them forget everything that has happened before today. They will no longer have a mean or hateful thought again. They will want to live in peace with all of us. This spell is cast now. It cannot be broken and will last forevermore.'

As the fairy dust was scattered, the yelling and shouting stopped in the hole. It became very quiet. At first, the fairies weren't sure the spell had worked. But soon they knew as the angels sang their sweet song.

The demons began to talk again, but now they sounded very different.

'What a beautiful day.'

'It's so nice to be all together.'

'Here, let me help you up.'

They acted like this was so natural for them. Once Balor was sure that the spell was indeed cast, he went right up to the edge of the big hole and told the leader that they would help them out.

'My, that's so nice of you. Thank you, dear dwarf.'

Koda was glad he'd had the foxes dig one last big tunnel with a stairway to the top so that the demons would be able to get out once the spell was cast. Balor and the other dwarfs were waiting at the top like a greeting committee.

As the demons began to climb out, it was almost as if they were seeing the dwarfs for the first time.

'Oh, thank you for the hand.'

'My, how sparkly you all are.'

'Oh, look at all the beautiful trees and flowers.'

'Maybe you can all come to our land and we will have a feast together.'

Just then, one of the demons noticed the little fairies flying all around.

'Oh look,' said one of the demons. 'Are those fairies?'

Arion flew close to him and spoke. 'Yes, we are fairies and we want to tell you how happy we are that we will all be sharing the same kingdom.'

'Oh yes,' replied the demon. 'That's great news.'

It was obvious that the demons really didn't remember how things used to be. It was like they were just coming here for the first time. And they seemed so happy about everything.

Just then, the foxes all gathered around. Balor told the demons how the foxes had built the stairway so that they could get out of the hole. Not one of the demons asked how they got into the hole, they just seemed grateful and happy to get out and meet all their *new* friends.

They all decided to accept the demons' invitation for a feast later that night."

"What about the mildrites?" cried Bidu. "Are they still in the jails? Did the demons forget them?"

Dartu laughed. "That's a great question, Bidu. The mildrites were still in the jails while the demons went to battle."

"What happened when the demons got back to their land and saw the mildrites?"

"Well, Bidu, why don't I just finish the story?" Dartu asked smiling.

Bidu settled back in her chair. She was still hanging on every word to see what happened to the mildrites.

Dartu began again.

"After all of the demons got out of the big hole, they headed back to their land. They knew where it was, but they didn't recognize much of it. There weren't many trees, or shrubs or flowers like there were in the other lands. It was more like a desert with a big stone castle in the middle and lots of walls all around it.

The demon leader, Varna (*Var-nah*), asked all the demons to gather around so that he could speak.

'Fellow demons, I am so happy that we have met our neighbors. I feel like we have lived alone for a long time. I can't remember much, but I felt a warmth and comfort when we went to visit our neighbors. Do you agree?'

All of the demons were nodding yes. None of them remembered that they went there to battle. The spell had worked very well.

'Let us go inside and prepare a feast for our neighbors.'

As they entered the big castle, they heard noises coming from underneath it.

'What is that?' asked Varna, but no one seemed to know.

'Let's go to see what that is all about.'

When they got downstairs, they saw the big jail with many prisoners, but the demons didn't remember any of them.

'What are you doing here?' asked Varna.

'You have kept us as prisoners for many years,' replied one of the mildrites.

'How awful,' said Varna. 'We don't want you to be prisoners. We want you to be friends.'

'You took us from our land, don't you remember?'

Varna thought as hard as he could, but he just couldn't remember. None of the demons could. He looked at the many mildrites in cages and he felt so bad. He gave the order to release all of the mildrites at once. He said to them, 'You are free to go to your own land, but first please stay with us for a big feast we are having tonight with our wonderful neighbors.'

The mildrites were completely confused. They wanted to run away once the cages were all opened, but something was so different. Besides, the demons had taken over all of their land, so they really didn't have any place to go. They weren't being treated as prisoners or as slaves or servants, but as friends. They were a very friendly tribe and this is what they had always wanted in the kingdom. So, they decided to stay and help with the feast. The demons helped too.

Soon, the dwarfs, the fairies and the foxes all arrived. There was lots of good food, music and dancing as though they had been friends since the beginning of time."

Bidu interrupted. "But how did the foxes come to be in Fairyland? I thought they all had their own land."

"That's a very good question," said Dartu. "Let me answer that."

"When they were all together at the feast, the foxes, the fairies and the dwarfs told the mildrites what had happened. They assured them that the demons would forever be kind and that they would be safe in their land. But the mildrites told them that the demons had taken all of their land and they had no place of their own anymore. All of the other lands in the kingdom were occupied by the dwarfs, the fairies and the foxes.

Arion thought for a while and then he talked to Koda.

'Koda, you know the dwarfs have a small land and there are so many dwarfs. They don't have any extra space. We fairies have a very big land and we are very little people. Perhaps the foxes would like to share our land and give your land to the mildrites?'

Koda thought about this. The foxes were always wanting to be closer to the others in the land, but for some reason, they were thought of as lower-level participants because they were "just animals." But this battle had made them much closer because they all worked together. They had formed a bond. And the foxes felt very protective of the fairies because they were so small. Koda took this idea to all of the foxes, and they all agreed. They would share our land and be our protectors."

"Oh!" cried Bidu. "So that's how the foxes came to be here!"

"That's right," Dartu said. "And it's been that way ever since. We all live together in harmony. We all help each other. And we still have wonderful feasts together."

"Can I go to the other lands?" asked Bidu.

Piru started to laugh. She knew Bidu so well.

"Oh, Daddy, can I take Bidu so she can meet everyone?"

Dartu was quiet. Bidu and Piru waited for what seemed like hours.

"I think that would be just fine," he said as he winked at Piru.

"There is a feast in two days. Now it's time for bed. Tomorrow we will talk about it and make some plans."

Bidu and Piru hugged each other and laughed and danced. There were no two happier fairies in all the land.

6

Lucinda

The day of the feast was finally here! Bidu was so excited that she would be seeing people from all of the lands Dartu had spoken about. She had so many questions for Piru.

"Piru, are the black-footed demons really nice now? Do they really have black feet? Do the demons and the mildrites really live in harmony now?"

Piru laughed until she fell to the floor rolling around. "Oh Bidu, you are so funny. Yes, it all happened just the way my father told it to you. I know it's hard to believe that everyone now helps each other, but it's true. You will see for yourself when we go to the feast. Everyone gets along and wants to do as much as they can for each other. It's just wonderful! And they will be very curious about you, but they will welcome you with loving open arms.....and yes, they really do have black feet!"

"I'm a little nervous," Bidu admitted.

"No need to worry," said Piru trying to reassure Bidu. "They will love you!"

Dartu's voice could be heard outside the girls' room.

"We'll be leaving in about ten minutes, so finish getting ready, girls."

"Yes, Daddy, we'll be ready," said Piru.

The girls were ready on time and Bidu was excited but still a little nervous. Piru was just excited to introduce Bidu to all of the other lands and beings in the kingdom.

All of a sudden, Bidu became very quiet and she seemed sad.

"What's wrong, Bidu?" asked Piru. "Are you OK?"

"Oh, I was just thinking about my parents. Are you sure they don't know I'm gone? They would be so worried if they did."

"Don't worry, my fairy sister. They are sleeping soundly with very sweet dreams. They have no idea you are gone."

"OK," said Bidu. She just needed some reassurance and she really did miss her parents. She would never want to make them worry or cause them any sadness.

"Come on, Bidu," Piru said excitedly. "Our rides are here. You're going to love this!"

The foxes were all lined up outside the fairy houses. Since the fairies were so small and lightweight, each fox could carry about ten of them at a time. Yes, the fairies could have flown to the feast, but the foxes liked to carry them and protect them, so the fairies let them do it. And the fairies loved bouncing up and down on the backs of the foxes. It was always such a fun ride!

Piru signaled Bidu to jump on the leader so that she would be up front and able to see everything on the way to the castle. The leader was Marmot, the strongest fox in the land. He knew his way all over the kingdom and he was very respected by all. He knelt so that the fairies could easily get on his back. Once they were all secure, he slowly rose up and began to walk toward the castle. They had to make their way all through Fairyland. Bidu was loving this ride because she could see all of the beautiful little cottages. The fairies really loved flowers and there were so many colorful flowers on the road. Blue, pink, red, yellow, purple… and so many combinations of all of the colors. Bidu was happy just looking at them all. Every cottage had a beautiful garden in front and each was different. Some had big flowering trees, and some had no trees, but lots of flowers. Some yards had both trees and flowers. Each one was different and they all were spectacular. Bidu loved everything she was seeing.

"Oh Piru!" cried Bidu. "I have never seen anything so beautiful! I feel so happy to be here."

"It's going to be an amazing day, Bidu. I'm so delighted to be taking you to the feast as my fairy sister."

Bidu and Piru smiled at each other. They both could feel the bond of love they shared. Piru was so happy to be sharing her world with Bidu, and all the while Bidu was thinking of every wonderful thing she wanted to share with Piru when they got back to human world.

As Marmot started up the hill, Bidu could see the castle up ahead. The top of it stuck up way over the big stone wall. As they got closer, she could hear festive music getting louder and louder. It was such happy music. Bidu couldn't sit still. She and Piru were moving to the music, and even Marmot began to sway from side to side so that they could feel it together. It was magical. As they got close to the entrance, they could see the bridge they had to cross.

Bidu asked, "Why is there no water in the moat below the bridge?"

Piru smiled. She was always so amazed at Bidu's excitement and reactions to things that were just ordinary to all of them. She tried to explain it to Bidu. "Moats were built to keep others out. The bridge used to be kept up so that no one could cross it. After the battle, there was no reason to have a moat anymore. But everyone loved the big bridge and the way it could go up and down, so they left it. The water finally dried up in the moat and there was never a reason to fill it again. Now it's just a reminder of the old days that no one ever wants to go back to."

As the foxes got closer to the bridge, they saw the dwarfs and the mildrites all arriving about the same time. Everyone was so courteous to each other.

"You first."

"No, you first."

It was such an orderly and kind procession as everyone tried to open the way for each other. So many smiles and so much happiness. Bidu couldn't believe that there ever could have been a battle here.

The music was playing and it seemed like everyone was dancing across the bridge instead of walking. Bidu felt an amazing joy as she glanced at Piru. She could see that Piru also felt the joy. Dartu reached out a hand to each of the girls and twirled them around right on Marmot's back. Bidu felt like this was one of the happiest days of her life. She wished her parents could be here too and she wondered if she would ever be able to describe this day to them so that they could truly feel it.

As they crossed the bridge into the courtyard, the demons were there to greet them with glasses of their special lemonade. It was pale blue. No one seemed to know what made it blue, but the flavor was beyond awesome. It tasted like lemonade, but there was something very special in the taste that could not be described. And just one sip filled each person with amazing joy. Bidu found out that this was a special recipe of the mildrites. Before the battle, the demons stole the recipe and would not let the mildrites make it anymore. But after the battle, and the spell that the fairies put on the demons, the demons tried to give the recipe back to the mildrites. They decided that they would share it and serve it only on special occasions and at every feast. It was amazing to see the demons and the mildrites working together and loving each other so much.

The dwarfs baked their special pinwheel pastries for dessert. They were full of berries and nuts, and everyone looked forward to them. Now, the dwarfs, foxes, mildrites, and demons knew that the fairies existed on fairy dust. So, the fairies didn't eat the food at the feasts, but they sure were happy to be there. And for some reason, they were able to sip a little of the blue lemonade and that was very special! Since everyone was watching out for each other and making sure that everyone was happy, they were all very accepting of one another and what worked for everyone.

The foxes laid down so the fairies could get down off them easily and then they all entered the big banquet hall. There were so many different looking beings! The demons were the tallest. To the fairies, dwarfs and foxes, they seemed like giants. To the mildrites they were more alike in height. The mildrites had red hair and blue eyes. The demons had black hair and dark eyes. Everyone was in a festive mood and the smells of the wonderful foods that had been prepared for the feast filled the air.

Piru took Bidu to everyone and told them of her story, how Bidu had saved her and was really a girl from human world.

They all wanted to know more about that because none of them had ever been to human world. They all gathered around Bidu and had so many questions for her about what it was like there. What did they eat? What did they do? Did they all look the same? Bidu did her best to answer all of their questions but with every answer came three more questions! Still, she kept answering as best she could. After all, in human world Bidu was just a normal 11-year-old girl. She didn't yet know everything about everything.

A huge gong sounded. It startled Bidu.

"Don't worry, Bidu," Piru reassured her. "It's just the big bell to let everyone know that dinner is served."

"Oh, OK," said Bidu. With that, they all started to line up at the huge buffet table. There were so many different foods and they were all laid out in such wonderful designs. Bidu loved the smells and wished she could taste some of the foods, but she wasn't a human girl right now. As a fairy, she had to be happy living on fairy dust and a few sips of the blue lemonade, but the smells reminded her of home and the wonderful foods her mother made every day.

"Oh, Piru, I can't wait to take you to human world as a girl so you can taste all the wonderful foods we have there. There is so much I want to show you!"

Right about then, Bidu noticed a demon staring at her and moving closer toward her and Piru.

"Piru," Bidu whispered. "There is a demon coming closer and she is staring at us."

"Don't worry, Bidu. Let's just talk with her. Everyone here is very friendly."

Piru spoke first. "Hello," she said. "I haven't seen you here before. What's your name?"

The demon girl was very shy. She just looked at the fairies, but she didn't speak. She looked at Bidu and Piru and then she looked down at the ground. Finally, she spoke. "Lucinda," she said softly. "My name is Lucinda."

"Why, that's a beautiful name," said Piru. "My name is Piru, and this is Bidu. Would you like to be friends?"

The demon girl nodded. Her black hair bounced as she moved her head. Then she smiled just a little bit. "We demons must wait until we are 11 years old before we can come to the feasts. This is my first feast."

Bidu smiled at her. "It's my first feast too. And I'm also 11 years old! I come from human world and Piru turned me into a fairy."

"Oh, I have heard that fairies can do magic. I wish I could see what it's like to be a fairy," said Lucinda.

"That's funny," said Piru. "I guess we all want to see what it's like to be something different. Tomorrow, I will go with Bidu to human world and I will see what it's like to be a human girl.

"Oh no!" cried Lucinda.

"What's the matter?" asked Bidu.

Lucinda seemed sad. "I just found you and now you are leaving tomorrow. I wish I could go too. Could I?"

"Gee, Lucinda," said Piru softly. I really don't know anything about being a human girl and I wouldn't be able to help you."

Bidu thought for a moment. "I'm so sorry Lucinda, but I will be taking Piru to my house for the first time. My parents don't even know that I have been turned into a fairy."

Lucinda started to cry. "I wouldn't be any trouble. I just want to have an adventure and see what it's like to be somewhere else."

"I understand," said Bidu. "But I don't think it will work this time. I'm sorry, Lucinda."

Lucinda wiped the tears from her eyes. She was disappointed, but she did understand. She was quiet for a few minutes and then she spoke. "OK, I get it. But if I can't go with you, could I at least come to say goodbye to you tomorrow before you go?"

"Of course," said both fairies at the same time. Then they all laughed.

"What time will you be going?" Lucinda asked.

Piru answered. "We will leave in the morning. Can you come to my house in Fairyland at nine o'clock tomorrow?"

"Oh yes!" cried Lucinda. "But I will go ask my mother right now." And with that she ran off and was gone for what seemed like a long time. When she returned, she was smiling and her mother was with her.

"I understand you fairies are taking a little trip tomorrow. Is that right?"

"Yes," said Piru. "We just met Lucinda and she wants to come to say goodbye to us in the morning. Would that be OK with you?"

Bidu just had to speak. "What if we took Lucinda home with us tonight so we could be together, and then after she says goodbye to us in the morning, we can have Marmot bring her back home?"

Lucinda's mother thought about it while Lucinda was jumping up and down.

"Oh, can I, Mother? Please. Oh please."

Lucinda's mother thought about it. She could see how much it would mean to her daughter.

"OK, Lucinda. I guess it will be all right. I know of Marmot and I trust he will bring you back home to me safely. But I do think you, Piru, should ask your parents if it's all right with them."

"Yes," said Piru. "I will ask them right now." Piru went to her parents and told them of this new development. Dartu had a concern.

"Will you be able to prepare all you need for your trip if you have Lucinda with you tonight? Maybe another time would be better?"

"Mama, Daddy, we know what we have to do for our journey. And we can still spend time with Lucinda."

They could see how excited Bidu and Piru were, and they knew that both girls were very responsible, so they said OK.

Now Lucinda, Bidu and Piru were all excited together.

Everyone enjoyed the rest of the feast. Bidu had never been to anything like it before in human world. Once she'd been to a wedding where there was lots of celebration and food, but it was nothing like the feast in this kingdom. She only secretly wished she was a girl right now so that she could taste all the yummy food that was everywhere. Piru didn't seem to mind not being able to eat. She was used to it. Bidu couldn't help but wonder what Piru would think when she was a human girl, eating human food, but she would find out soon enough.

After a wonderful evening of food, lemonade, music and dancing, it was time to go. Lucinda seemed so excited. She had no fear about leaving the castle and going to Fairyland. She reminded Bidu of herself… always looking for an adventure to see and learn new things. She felt close to Lucinda even though they had only just become new friends.

Marmot was there, ready to take Bidu and Piru back to their home. Lucinda would have to walk alongside because she was too heavy to ride on Marmot. She didn't seem to mind. She was too excited about what was to come. And it wasn't a long ride from the castle to Fairyland. Lucinda kissed her mother and thanked her for letting her go. Her mother gave her a big, long hug and told her to have a good time.

"I'll see you in the morning after you say goodbye to your new friends."

Lucinda nodded, but it was as if she had a plan of her own…

Soon they arrived back at Piru's cottage. This posed a bit of a problem, because Lucinda couldn't get through the door! She was way too big. Luckily, it was a nice warm night and Lucinda was happy to sleep out under the stars. A pack of foxes curled up around her to keep her warm and she was very happy.

Morning came quickly. The sun shone on Lucinda and woke her up. She tapped on the door of Piru's cottage, and the fairies came out to greet her. Lucinda was hungry, but she already knew that fairies only ate fairy dust. The foxes knew that too, so Marmot went out hunting and brought back some nuts and berries for Lucinda.

Dartu and Lila were a bit concerned about their little girl going to human world. They knew Bidu and they trusted her, but still they had some apprehension.

"Piru, what exactly is the plan for this visit to human world?" asked Lila.

Piru began to explain. "Bidu will need to be released from the spell of being a fairy so that she can once again be a human girl. Then, somehow I will need to become a human girl too. Daddy, could you please do that for us so that it's all for good?"

"Yes, of course, Piru. It most certainly will be for good, because I know you girls will be helpful wherever you are."

Lila was concerned. "How will you preserve your fairy powers in case you need them?"

Dartu had a suggestion. "I think you should keep your fairy wings in case you need them. Once you have transformed into girls, you will be big and the fairy wings won't really show much on your back, but they will still be there when and if you need them."

"Oh, Daddy!" cried Piru. "That's a great idea."

Dartu continued. "And I think it might be good for you to spin a bunch of fairy dust before you go, so you have it ready in case you need it. You can use my special necklace of small bead containers that can hold lots of fairy dust."

Lila added, "And Bidu, I also have a necklace of beads that will hold fairy dust for you as well. I will feel better if I know you are protected in every way. How long do you think you'll be gone?"

"Only a few days, I think," said Piru. "What do you think, Bidu?"

"Yes, a few days sounds right. There is so much I want to show you, but we'll try not to be gone more than 2 or 3 days. Is that OK?"

Lila would miss her daughter, but she was happy that she would be having a new and wonderful experience. And she was glad that she had found Bidu.

"I think that will be fine," Lila said. "I'll miss you, but I do want you to have a wonderful visit. Your father and I will be waiting to see you and hear all about it."

Lucinda was listening to every word. Oh how she wished she could be going too. She tried to talk to the girls one more time, and although they thought it would be fun to all go together, they decided that they should just stay with the original plan.

It was time to get going. Piru asked her daddy to do the spell for her and Bidu to become human girls and bless them with good luck so that their trip would be successful.

Lucinda watched and listened as Dartu spoke.

"Sweet spirits, return Bidu to the beautiful girl she was in human world. Give her all the loving attributes she had then. Take all of those loving attributes and mix them with the special qualities of Piru. Let them blossom as you turn Piru into a human girl as well. Let them keep their fairy wings and maintain their ability to make fairy dust which they will use for only good. Guide them on a safe journey and return Piru to us safe and sound. Amen."

"Amen," said Bidu.

"Amen," said Piru.

Even Lucinda said, "Amen." She watched as both Bidu and Piru became human girls. They stood next to each other and they were exactly the same size as Lucinda! As fairies, the black-footed demons seemed like giants, but once they were human girls, they were all the same size. They were so amazed! There were lots of hugs and happiness.

Lucinda was thinking as she said to the girls, "I will walk you to the end of Fairyland. I know how to get back to the castle. I don't need Marmot to take me."

Piru thought for a moment. She had promised Lucinda's mother that she would get Lucinda home. "Daddy?" Piru asked. "Do you think it would be OK for Lucinda to walk us to the boundary line?"

Dartu looked at Lucinda and asked, "Lucinda, do you know the way back?"

"Oh yes, I do," said Lucinda. "I have wandered out many times before and I know my way around. If you want, I can come back here once the girls cross over to human world so that Marmot can take me the rest of the way."

"OK then, Lucinda. We will wait here for you to come back. Marmot will be ready. It's a short walk to the boundary for human land, so it shouldn't take very long. You girls be safe and stay together. The spell will only last while you are on your journey. Remember, you cannot come back to Fairyland or you will instantly be turned back into fairies and your journey will be over."

"Yes, Daddy," said Piru.

Bidu was getting excited to see her parents. She was also excited to show Piru around human world.

They began their walk to the end of the boundary with Lucinda. It was only about a 20-minute walk and it went too fast for Lucinda. Once they were at the boundary, Bidu and Piru hugged Lucinda. Then it was time to say their goodbyes. They went in their separate directions, turning to wave a few times.

Once Bidu and Piru stopped turning around, Lucinda scurried behind a tree and watched to see where the girls were going.

Bidu turned one more time, but couldn't see Lucinda.

"Well, I guess she's on her way," she said to Piru.

"Yes," Piru agreed. "Maybe one day we can all have an adventure together."

"Oh yes, that would be wonderful," said Bidu.

Then the girls continued on their journey.

"So, Piru, how does it feel to be a human girl?" asked Bidu.

"I feel big," said Piru, "and I think I'm hungry. My stomach feels like it's growling."

Bidu laughed. "Yup! You're human now. Wait until we get home to my house. My mother is a wonderful cook and you will love eating!"

Meanwhile, Lucinda was hiding behind trees trying to follow the girls, but the girls were so busy talking and laughing that they never heard her.

All of a sudden, there was a scream. Bidu and Piru turned to see where it was coming from. They saw Lucinda jump out from behind a tree.

"Help me! Help me! There's a bunch of monsters here!"

Bidu and Piru knew they couldn't turn back or they would become fairies again. Lucinda was hysterical. She was surrounded by a family of hedgehogs.

"Oh, Lucinda," yelled Bidu. "Those are only hedgehogs. They are human world animals and they won't hurt you. We can't come to get you or the spell will be broken. What are you doing here? You're supposed to be on your way home."

Lucinda ran towards the girls. Now they were all together. The hedgehogs followed Lucinda, surrounding all of the girls.

"Don't be afraid girls. The hedgehogs are just curious, but they won't harm us."

"I'm OK," said Piru. Then she looked at Lucinda.

"Lucinda, your parents will be waiting for you. And we will all get into trouble for not keeping our word."

Bidu was thinking. Then she spoke. "Piru, is there any way you can put a spell on Lucinda's parents from here so that they are sleeping while she is gone?"

"I've never done a long-distance spell before, but I know it can be done. It requires a lot of our fairy dust though and we don't want to use it up too fast."

"Since we saved our wings, can't we make more fairy dust?" Bidu asked.

"I think it might work," said Piru. "And we don't need to put any spells on Lucinda because she's the same size we are."

"Oh, Piru, can we?" cried Lucinda. "Please. Oh, please."

Piru looked at Bidu. Bidu looked at Piru. They both looked at Lucinda and her pleading eyes.

Finally, Piru agreed. She would do a long-distance spell on Lucinda's parents so that they would not know their daughter was gone. She would have to do the spell as a gift to Lucinda's parents so they wouldn't worry and in that way it would be for good.

All three girls held hands as Piru cast the spell. She opened one of her beads and held the fairy dust up in the air as she said, "Sweet spirits, take this dust to the castle and sprinkle it on Lucinda's parents. Let them fall into a deep slumber until their daughter returns. Keep them safe and protected and surrounded in this fairy dust. And so it is."

Bidu and Lucinda both said, "And so it is."

The angels sang, so Bidu and Piru felt safe that the spell had worked.

"We need to get going," said Piru. "Bidu, please tell us everything we need to know about your parents and your world while we are on our way."

Bidu started to tell them everything she thought was important, when suddenly, just as they entered the town, a man rushed past and crashed into them. He kept going like a bullet, but on the ground, he left something very strange...

7

The Enchanted Clock

Lucinda was lying on the ground. She had been hit directly by the runaway man. Piru and Bidu went to help her up. They were all pretty shaken by the scary incident.

"What was that?" asked Lucinda. "And what's that over there on the ground?"

"Let's take a closer look," said Bidu. Piru bent down to pick it up. Bidu took hold of her arm.

"No, wait!" Bidu exclaimed. The other girls stopped. They understood that Bidu knew the ways of human world and they did not. They waited for Bidu to take a look first. She knelt next to what the man had dropped as he ran past them. She looked closely at what looked like a funny kind of clock. She had never seen anything like it before. It had the face of a clock, but the numbers were different. There were other buttons and lights and

94

little sliding doors in many colors that Bidu didn't recognize. And there was a dial so that it could dial to any of the funny numbers right next to a small keyboard. Something on the face looked like a compass, but it wasn't a compass.

"I think we need to take this to a clock shop," said Bidu. "This looks like a clock, sort of, but it's also very different. My father has a friend who has a store with all kinds of clocks. He might know what this one is. But first I would like to take it home and let my father see it."

"Bidu," said Piru. "First we have to wake your parents up from their sleep and then you have to tell them about me."

"And me," said Lucinda.

"Oh my," said Bidu. "Yes, you are right. Let's go to sit on that bench over there for a minute."

The girls went together to the bench as Bidu was talking.

"I have to think about what I'm going to tell my parents. It seems like a lot and I do have to tell them the truth about everything."

The girls sat and let Bidu have a moment of quiet to gather her thoughts. After a few minutes, Bidu spoke. "Piru, when my parents wake up, will it be just like nothing has happened at all?"

"Yes, Bidu. Remember that I put the spell on them so when they went to bed that night, it would be just like they had a great night of sleep. They will wake up refreshed and happy. But when they look at the calendar, they will see that 5 days have passed! And they might be a little surprised to see two new, strange girls in their house!"

Bidu had an idea. "I have a very big, cool tree house that my daddy built for me. It's in the back yard."

Lucinda interrupted. "What's a tree house?"

Bidu laughed. "I forgot that you aren't really human girls. A tree house is a house built in a tree. When we get back, you two can just wait there while I'm talking to my parents. Piru, what do I need to do to wake them up?"

Piru answered, "I will go inside with you at first and break the spell. Then Lucinda and I will go to the tree house while you talk with them."

"Oh, I hope they're not mad at me for being gone so long."

Piru reminded her. "Remember, they have no idea that you have been gone at all!"

"Oh yes," said Bidu. "I guess I'm just nervous about what to say exactly."

"Not to worry, fairy sister. I have that covered! Let's go to your house and you will see that it will all be OK."

The girls walked together in silence for the last few blocks on the way to Bidu's house. As they approached the house, Bidu said, "This is where I live. Let's go!"

When they got to the front door, it was locked.

"Oh no!" cried Bidu. "We can't get in."

"Bidu," Piru said softly. "You need to calm down. Remember when we left, we flew out of your bedroom window?"

"Oh yes, now I remember. Let's go around to the back where my bedroom is."

The girls followed Bidu. The window was open about five inches… just the right amount for a fairy to fly through.

Just then, Bidu looked at Piru. "Oh, Piru, what a wonderful journey we've had."

"Yes," said Piru. "And now we will have another wonderful but different journey as girls and we can share it with Lucinda."

"Yes, you're right, Piru," said Bidu. With that she extended her hands to both of the girls. As they all held hands, Bidu said, "I'm so glad to have met you both and I'm so happy we are together now."

Lucinda smiled. Piru smiled. Bidu smiled too.

They all walked around to the back of the house.

Lucinda cried out, "Oh look! Is that your tree house? It's so awesome! It looks like a real house!"

"Yes, that's it!" said Bidu.

"Wait till you see the inside, but first let's go into my bedroom. Give me a hand, girls. Let's open up this window!"

She was more certain, more confident now.

There was a bench on the back porch. They moved it right under the window, then climbed up and pushed the window open wide enough for them to climb through. First Bidu, then Piru, then Lucinda.

Once they were all in the bedroom, Bidu told the girls to follow her to the kitchen. She wanted to get them some snacks to take to the tree house. She packed some apples, some cheese and some rice crackers. Then she asked Piru to reverse the spell on her parents. They all stood in the doorway to Bidu's parents' bedroom.

Piru put her hands up to signal to the girls to be very quiet as she spoke. "Dear spirits, gently wake these sleeping angels. Let them wake with love and joy in their hearts. And let Bidu find just the right words to share her adventure with them. They will awaken with a kiss from their daughter and the spell will be broken."

"Now," said Piru. "We can go to the tree house until you come for us."

"Let me take you there," said Bidu. She led the way as they climbed the ladder to the tree house. It was so amazing inside. There was a pink carpet and pink ruffled curtains. It looked like a dollhouse in a tree! But it was big enough for all three girls to be inside together.

There was a white table, and four white chairs with pink cushion seats in the kitchen and four big pink and white beanbag chairs in the living room. There was a balcony off the living room with a big pink swing to rock in. Bidu had so many happy moments in this tree house over the years, and now she was so happy to be sharing it with Piru and Lucinda.

"Make yourselves comfortable, girls. I'll be back soon. Piru, I hope you enjoy your first human food! And Lucinda, I know you have eaten apples and cheese because I saw both of those things at the feast, but have you ever had rice crackers?"

"I don't think so," said Lucinda as she reached for one. As she took the first bite she said, "Oh, these are yummy and crunchy! You go ahead, Bidu. I'll take care of Piru."

Bidu felt fine to leave them, so she went down the ladder back to the house and tiptoed to her parents' bedroom. She went over to her mother first. She always thought her mama was so pretty. She had soft brown curls and deep brown eyes. And she always had a smile. Bidu could feel the love every time her mama looked at her. She slowly bent down to kiss her softly on her cheek. Her mother began to stir.

Then Bidu went to the other side of the bed and looked at her daddy. He was always so nice. His voice was soft and reassuring. He had short dark hair. His eyes were hazel, and they were such kind eyes. Bidu kissed her daddy softly. He yawned and began to stretch.

Both of her parents opened their eyes and saw their precious daughter.

"Good morning, Bidu," said her mother.

"Good morning, sweetheart," said her father.

"Oh, I'm so happy to see you both!" cried Bidu. She hugged her daddy for a long time and then went back to the other side of the bed and hugged her mother.

Bidu's mother began to laugh. "What's all this?" she asked. "You act as though you haven't seen us for a long time."

Bidu knew it HAD been a long time, but for a moment she forgot that her parents didn't know anything... yet.

"I have so much to tell you," said Bidu. "Are you fully awake now?"

"Bidu, I'd really love to have a cup of coffee," said her mother. "Why don't we talk in the kitchen. Let Daddy and I get dressed and we'll be right there."

"OK," said Bidu. She went into the kitchen and started the coffee. Bidu didn't really like to drink coffee, but she knew how to make it just right, the way her parents liked it.

Soon after the coffee was brewing, her parents came into the kitchen. They always sat in the same seats, and this morning was no exception. Bidu served the coffee to her parents, then poured a glass of orange juice for herself.

"So, Bidu," said her mother. "You seem to have something you want to share with us."

"Oh yes," said Bidu. "So much, I'm not sure where to begin."

"Did you have a bad dream?" asked her father.

"Oh no, Daddy," said Bidu. "This is way better than a dream!"

"Why not just start at the beginning?" said her mother.

Bidu took a deep breath. She loved her parents so much. She wanted to say everything just right so that they would feel like they had been on the journey with her.

She began slowly, starting with the afternoon that she had come home late. That was the day she found Piru. It seemed like a long time ago now. "Let me tell you everything," she said. "Then when I'm done, I will answer all of your questions. Some of this will sound like it couldn't possibly happen, but I promise you every word is true."

Bidu talked and talked. She could see the disbelief on her parents' faces as she told them how she had found Piru, how she helped mend her wing and how Piru changed her into a fairy. She told them how Piru cast a spell on them so that Bidu could take her home. She told them of the fairy snatchers, and how they escaped. She told them of the other kingdom next to human world, of the fairies, the dwarfs, the foxes, the mildrites, and the black-footed demons. Her parents tried not to interrupt, but it was all so unbelievable. Bidu wasn't one to make up stories and they could tell that something was so different about her, that maybe this story could actually be real. Bidu seemed older, more mature. So, they continued to listen.

Bidu went on to tell of the story Dartu had told, about the way it was before the battle, and how the battle changed everything. She tried to remember every word that Dartu had said as she relayed every detail of the journey she could remember. She told them all about the feast, and how Piru's father changed them back to girls so that she could come back to human world with Bidu.

Bidu's mother couldn't stay silent one more second. "Bidu, that's a great story, but are you saying all of this happened in just one night?"

Bidu laughed. "Oh no, Mama. I was gone for 5 days. Piru put a spell on you and Daddy. You slept the entire time."

Bidu's father finally spoke. "Now, Bidu, you do have an amazing imagination, but I really don't think anyone could sleep for 5 days!"

"You could if a fairy cast a spell on you and sprinkled you with fairy dust. You see this necklace I'm wearing right now? It's full of fairy dust. But we can only use it for good. Oh, there is still so much more to tell. But first, go and get your calendar and you will see that 5 days have passed."

Bidu felt that was the best way to prove that she was indeed telling the truth.

Her mother went to the cabinet where the calendar always hung.

"Oh, my goodness!" she shouted. "Yes, it has been 5 days!"

Her father seemed more interested now. "Bidu, where did you stay in this other kingdom?"

Bidu continued. "I stayed in Piru's house while I was in Fairyland and I was a real fairy while I was there. I wanted to bring Piru back with me so she could see what it's like to be a human girl and her parents said it was OK. So Piru's father changed me back to myself, and then changed Piru into a girl too."

"Well, Bidu, where is she now?" asked her father.

"She's waiting in the tree house. She wanted me to be able to tell you everything. She can't wait to meet you. I know you will love her too. Just remember that she has only been a human girl for one day. And fairies only eat fairy dust, so she hasn't ever had human food. Mama, could you make chicken and noodles for dinner tonight?"

Her mother laughed. "Yes of course, Bidu. We will take good care of your guest. Why don't you go get her now?"

"Well… there's more to tell first," Bidu said. She took a deep breath and went on. She told them of how they met Lucinda and how she'd followed them, and that once she was in human world, they couldn't turn back.

"Lucinda is also in the tree house right now," said Bidu.

"Oh my," said her mother. "Just how many people are waiting in the tree house?"

Bidu smiled at her mother. "Only Piru and Lucinda."

Bidu's father looked at her mother. Then he looked at Bidu.

"Well then, I think it's time to bring the other girls in."

Her mother nodded in agreement.

Bidu so wanted to tell them about the clock they'd found, but she decided to wait until her parents met the other girls. She had told them so much. It sounded so unreal, even to Bidu as she listened to herself tell the story. But it couldn't have been more true.

"OK," said Bidu. "You wait here and I'll go get the girls."

Bidu ran to get them. As she got closer to the tree house, she could hear the girls giggling. She was glad they were having fun because she had been gone for a long time. As she climbed the ladder, she called up to the girls. "I'm back, girls."

Piru answered first. "I love apples! I never had one before. They're delicious. And this tree house is so amazing!"

Bidu had never heard Piru sound so excited.

"Lucinda, are you OK?" asked Bidu.

"Oh yes!" exclaimed Lucinda. "I love it here. Did you talk to your parents?"

"Yes," said Bidu. "They can't wait to meet you. Let's go to the house. They are waiting for you."

The girls headed down the ladder and across the lawn. They could feel the warmth as soon as they entered the kitchen. Bidu's mother spoke first. "Hello, girls. We are so happy you are here."

"Yes, welcome," said Bidu's father. "You can call me Jim and Bidu's mother is Marie. Now, which one of you is Piru?"

Piru stepped forward. Jim thought she looked like a fairy with her long blonde hair and sparkling blue eyes.

"And you must be Lucinda," he said. He knew from Bidu's story that she was something called a 'black-footed demon'. She looked a lot like a human girl although he had never seen hair so black. Even her eyes were black, but they were soft and friendly.

"Come and sit down," said Marie. "Can I get you something to drink?"

"Mama, could we have hot chocolate? I don't think either of the girls have ever had a hot chocolate," said Bidu.

"Of course," said Marie. "Should I put a marshmallow in it too?"

Piru asked, "What's a mishmarshall?"

Bidu burst out laughing. "It's a marsh-mell-o." Bidu tried to pronounce it in syllables.

"Yes, Mama, please put in 'mishmarshalls'!" Bidu had a feeling she would never again be able to say marshmallow, only mishmarshall. And it was fun to say it!

Marie served the hot chocolate and the girls loved it!

Bidu's parents seemed truly happy to have all the girls there and they had lots of questions, which the girls seemed happy to answer.

Bidu's mother asked, "What's the best part of coming to human world so far?"

Piru answered first. "Being a real girl... I feel so big! Oh, and eating human food. This hot chocolate is delicious! And the mishmarshall is yummy!"

Lucinda agreed as she took another big gulp of her hot chocolate and all three girls giggled.

"Wait until you taste my mama's chicken and noodles for dinner... that will be a super treat!" said Bidu.

"What about you, Lucinda? Do you have a favorite part?"

Lucinda blurted out, "Finding the strange clock, but I didn't like being knocked down!"

"What strange clock? I don't remember Bidu mentioning that." said Jim. "You mean there is still more to the story?"

"Oh, Daddy," said Bidu. "Yes, there is one more thing."

Bidu went on to tell them how the man crashed into them and left behind a very weird looking clock. Then she went into her bedroom where she had left it when they had come through the window. She came back holding the clock.

"What do you think of this, Daddy? What could it be? It looks like a clock… sort of, but it's not really a clock. What do you think it is?"

Jim gently took the clock and looked at it very closely. He could see that Bidu had described it perfectly. It had a lot of unusual things on it that he didn't recognize ever seeing on a clock before.

"Bidu," he said. "I think we should take this to Mr. Mayer. He is my friend and he knows all about clocks. He has had his clock store for many years and he has seen many different clocks. Let's see what he says."

"Oh, that's a great idea, Daddy. When can we go?" asked Bidu.

"How about right now, girls?" answered Jim. "I know you're all excited to see if this is anything, so let's end the suspense and go find out."

Marie agreed. "Why don't all of you go to see Mr. Mayer, and I'll stay here. I have an important assignment too. I have to make chicken and noodles for you all." She looked at Bidu with that warm, tender look she had. Bidu was happy to be home again, but still she was so excited to know more about this clock – or whatever it was.

The town was just a short walk from Bidu's house, so they all set out on foot. The sun was shining and it was a lovely day for a walk. As they made their way into town, everyone seemed to know Bidu and her father.

"Hello, Jim, beautiful day, eh?"

"Hey there, Bidu, how are you doing?"

When they passed by the ice cream store, the owner, Carl, came out to say hello and ask who Bidu's new friends were. Bidu introduced Piru and Lucinda.

"Where are you girls from?" Carl asked.

Jim decided to step in and answer. "Bidu met these girls at summer camp and they are visiting for a while." Then he winked at Bidu. Her daddy always seemed to know just what to say and do.

"Well," said Carl. "Welcome and enjoy your stay. And don't forget to come back while you're here and have a free ice cream."

"What's ice cream?" asked Piru.

Bidu kept forgetting that Piru had no idea of any of the food things that she was so familiar with.

Lucinda asked, "Yes, what's ice cream?" She had never heard of it either.

"Oh girls, you are in for a real treat! I won't say another word, you can just taste for yourselves."

Jim had something to say. "I think we should save that for tomorrow. Let's save our appetites for your mother's amazing dinner."

"Yes, you're right, Daddy," said Bidu as they continued walking to Mr. Mayer's clock shop, which wasn't much of a walk now as it was only two doors down from Carl's ice cream shop.

Bidu could feel her heart beat faster. She was really excited to find out about this clock. She had a feeling it was going to be something special. She didn't know exactly what it would be but somehow, she felt an adventure coming. Sometimes she would get a 'feeling' and more often than not she was right. Her mother always told her she had special intuition.

"I'm so excited to find out what this is," Bidu exclaimed.

"Me too," said Piru.

"Me three!" said Lucinda as she started laughing at her joke.

All the girls started to giggle. Even Jim laughed. It was good to see all the girls so happy.

"Here we are," said Jim. "Let's go to see what Mr. Mayer has to say."

They all went into the shop. So many clocks were on the walls and on the tables. They were all different sizes and colors and there was a big cuckoo clock right next to the door. Mr. Mayer was busy talking to a police officer. He looked concerned, but he still stopped to speak to Jim and Bidu.

"Hey there, Jim. I'll just be a minute more. Hi Bidu! Why don't you and your little friends look around for a bit and I'll be right with you as soon as I can."

The girls had fun looking around. All of a sudden, the cuckoo clock began to chime and then the door swung open and out came a big cuckoo bird squawking, "Cuckoo, Cuckoo."

It made Piru jump. She had never seen anything like that in Fairyland. Oh, they had clocks, but nothing fancy like in here! And Lucinda was laughing because she thought the cuckoo clock was so funny. In fact, Lucinda laughed a lot. Once Piru saw that there was nothing to be afraid of, she started to laugh too, and then of course, Bidu had to join in. Jim was enjoying how well the girls got along and how much fun it was to show them things they had never seen before.

After a few minutes, the police officer left the store and Mr. Mayer came over to them. He looked worried.

"What's the matter, John?" Jim asked. Mr. Mayer's first name was John, but all the children called him Mr. Mayer out of respect for him.

"Oh, Jim, I was robbed last night."

"Oh no!" said Jim. "What happened? Did anyone get hurt?"

"No, luckily no one was here. But they took about 10 of my most special and valuable clocks. I wonder if it's someone who knew what I have here in the store."

Jim was surprised. This was a very safe town and hardly any crimes were ever committed here.

"Do you know exactly what was taken?" Jim asked.

"Yes. I keep a very tight inventory and I know every clock that is missing."

Jim looked at Bidu. "I think you should tell Mr. Mayer what happened to you today and show him what you found."

Bidu felt so bad for Mr. Mayer. She really wanted to keep this clock, but she knew if it was one of the clocks that had been stolen, she would have to give it back. She began to tell her story about the man who ran into them and dropped something on the ground.

"It looks like a clock, but then it doesn't look like any clock I have ever seen," said Bidu. With that she took the clock out of the paper bag she had been carrying it in.

"Oh, my!" gasped Mr. Mayer. "That is my most special clock! It was not for sale and was never out in my store. It was always in the back in a special cabinet. Did you get a good look at the man who dropped it?"

"I'm so sorry, Mr. Mayer, but he was running so fast and he ran right into us, so we didn't see his face at all."

"Bidu, think. Do you remember anything about him? Anything at all?"

"Well…" Bidu said as she thought about it. "I think he had a blue baseball cap on. And he was carrying a big brown bag. Do you think he had the other clocks in that bag?"

"That's a very good possibility, Bidu. I think you were run into by the thief. Where were you when he ran into you?"

"We were at the big park by the lake."

"Where exactly at the park?" asked Mr. Mayer.

"By the soccer field. If you want to go there, I can show you exactly where it was."

"Thank you, Bidu. You have been a huge help. I think I'll have you talk to the police and we will let them investigate. Now let me have a look at it please."

Bidu handed the clock to Mr. Mayer, but really she didn't want to part with it. He held it like it was a baby… so gently and so carefully.

"Let's see if any of the parts are missing." He laid it down on a table and looked it over and over. First, he just looked with his regular glasses. Then, he got out a magnifying glass and studied it. "I think there is one small spring that is missing, but I can fix that no problem," he said. "You know, this is an enchanted clock and if it ever got into the wrong hands, it could be devastating."

"What do you mean?" asked Bidu.

"This clock has magic powers. It can allow you to time travel to any place and any time in the past, present, or future if you know how to use it. It can help you or it can hurt you depending on what your motivation and intentions are."

"Oh," said Piru. "Is it like fairy dust?"

"What do you know of fairy dust?" asked Mr. Mayer.

"Well, fairy dust, when in the hands of fairies can only be used for good. If bad people get hold of it, they can try to use it just for themselves. We have to keep it very protected."

"My, my," said Mr. Mayer, "you sure know a lot about fairies."

Bidu decided it was time for her to say something. "Yes, Mr. Mayer, we have studied fairies and fairy literature. It's really interesting."

"That's nice, Bidu." Mr. Mayer was more interested in his enchanted clock, so it was easy to distract him.

"Tell me, John," Jim said, "What else did the thief take?"

"He took some of my most expensive clocks, some with diamonds and other precious stones in them. But none with the powers of this one."

"Mr. Mayer, do you think you have the right spring for the enchanted clock? I'd really like to see how it works," said Bidu.

"Just wait here for a minute. I will go in the back to my workstation and I will see what I can do. Jim, please keep an eye on the store and let me know if anyone comes in."

"Will do, John."

Mr. Mayer slipped away but he was only gone for about 10 minutes. The girls looked around at all the clocks wondering if each one had a story. But mostly, they wanted to know more about the enchanted clock.

"OK, girls," said Mr. Mayer as he came out from the back of the store. "I think it's good as new."

Bidu just had to ask. "Why do you call it enchanted? Can you really time travel with it? Have you ever time traveled with it?"

"Whoa, whoa, Bidu." Mr. Mayer held his hand up. "Not so fast. I will tell you everything about this clock and I will answer all of your questions." Bidu, Piru, and Lucinda moved as close to Mr. Mayer as they could. Jim was very interested in hearing everything as well. A hush fell over the store as Mr. Mayer began to speak. "I call it enchanted because of all the magical things it can do. And yes, you can really time travel with it."

Bidu interrupted. "Did you ever try to time travel?" she asked.

"Yes, I have," Mr. Mayer said. "Let's just say that this truly is an enchanted clock. And in the right hands will provide amazing adventures. It's like a being of its own. If you treat it right and it feels your goodness, it will respond to you. It won't ever respond to tyrants, or criminals, or monsters. It can tell the difference. I have cared for this clock for all these years, and I have asked little in return."

"That's amazing!" said Jim.

"Yes, it is," said Mr. Mayer. "Jim, I would like to give a little reward to Bidu and her friends for finding and returning this clock. Perhaps a hundred dollars would do?"

"That's a lovely gesture," said Jim.

"Mr. Mayer?" said Bidu. "I have another idea if you don't mind."

"Whatever could that be, Bidu?" He was a little surprised at the boldness of this little girl, but he did want to hear what she had to say.

Lucinda and Piru also wanted to hear what Bidu had to say. And Jim was watching and waiting to hear as well.

Mr. Mayer knew that he never would have recovered this clock without her and her little friends so he extended the courtesy of hearing her out.

"Go ahead, Bidu. What is your idea?"

Bidu wasn't sure exactly how to say what she wanted to say, but she could hear her parents and how they always told her to speak her heart. She took a deep breath and began.

"Mr. Mayer, I have always believed in magic and fairies and enchanted things. I know I'm still very young, but I have actually had a few experiences in the spiritual world that a lot of people would not believe to be true, just like I suppose many people would not believe that this clock is truly enchanted."

"Yes, Bidu. When I first got this clock, I told a few people about it. They looked at me like I was crazy. I had to stop telling others of this clock, so I do understand what you are saying."

Bidu went on. "I appreciate that you want to give me money for returning this clock, but with all due respect, sir, instead of money, I would really like to know this clock and have an experience with it."

"What exactly do you mean?" asked Mr. Mayer.

"I would like you to tell me more about how this clock is enchanted and how I might time travel with it."

Piru, Lucinda and Jim were listening intently to every word that Bidu was saying. They couldn't believe she was asking to time travel. Although Jim was apprehensive, he was just starting to believe in some of the things that Bidu had always known to be true.

Of course, Piru and Lucinda believed everything was possible because after all, their kingdom had fairies!

Mr. Mayer stayed quiet and let Bidu talk.

"I promise I will take good care of the clock. I already feel like I know it. Please, Mr. Mayer. Will you show me how to time travel?" Bidu looked up at him with her big brown eyes.

"Bidu, I have known you since you were born. You have always been a special girl… kind, loving, and always very dependable and responsible. But time travel can be dangerous. You never know what you will find once you get to where you are traveling."

Bidu's daddy was feeling a little nervous. "Actually, Bidu, I think perhaps you're a little young to be undertaking such an adventure. Maybe it would be better when you're a little older."

"Oh, Daddy, Piru and Lucinda are only here for a little while. You know the adventures we've already had and we've come through them just fine. I promise you, we would be so careful. Besides, you always say that I am divinely protected. I believe that Mr. Mayer can show me everything I need to know. And besides, we have Piru with us and you know what that means."

Bidu then covered her mouth so that only her daddy could see it and whispered, "Fairy dust!"

"I don't know, sweetheart," said her daddy.

"Can't you just show it to me, Mr. Mayer… please."

Mr. Mayer looked to Jim for a sign. Jim nodded his head slowly. He did know that Bidu could handle many things, but after all, she was only 11. And now she had the extra responsibility of watching out for Piru and Lucinda.

Mr. Mayer handed the clock to Bidu. He could tell by the way she held it that she would be careful with it.

"OK, Bidu. Listen carefully. And you other girls listen closely too in case Bidu forgets anything."

They all gathered around Mr. Mayer as he began to explain every detail. He explained everything. He showed her how to set the dials for the year she wanted to go to, but the secret was that she had to enter the year backwards. Then she had to enter the location she wanted to go to. First, she would have to push the green button, and that would open up the screen to type. If you didn't know this, you would never be able to find it on the clock. And, she would have to type the location in backwards too.

"So, Bidu. Let's say you do get to have an adventure with this clock. Where would you like to go?"

Bidu thought about it for a minute. "In school, we have studied Cleopatra and Egypt. Could we go there?"

"You can go anywhere with this clock, but the days of Cleopatra were over 2000 years ago. Maybe you want to start with something a little closer in time?"

"I feel very strongly that Egypt is the right place. Can I try to put the information into the clock just to be sure I understand?"

Mr. Mayer looked at Jim again for a sign. Bidu could see that Mr. Mayer was waiting for her daddy to nod.

"Please, Daddy," Bidu pleaded. "Can't I..."

Mr. Mayer interrupted. "There is something else you should know," he said. "You will need to keep this clock with you at all times in this bag." He pulled out a purple velvet bag with a shoulder strap. "You need to keep this clock protected and out of sight in the bag. Never take it off, even when you are sleeping. If ever there is danger, the clock will sound an alarm. Only you will be able to hear the alarm. This clock will try to guide you all the way. Once the alarm sounds, slide this little blue door and the clock will send you a message that only you will be able to read. It will be cryptic to anyone else, but you will know exactly what the message says. And never ever take it all the way out of the bag. Take it out like this," said Mr. Mayer, as he showed her how to keep the clock in the bag, and still expose only the face.

Bidu watched closely. Then she asked, "By the way, does this clock have a name?"

"A very important question, Bidu. This clock is named Gregor. He likes to feel you close at all times.

He will be able to feel your mood or if you are in danger. If there is an emergency and you need to come back immediately, you just need to call his name three times. He will bring you back to where you were when you started, which is here. You don't have to take the time to enter all of the information. Do you understand?"

"Yes," said Bidu. "I understand everything. Can I try to enter the information now?"

"Hold on, Bidu. There's more." Mr. Mayer looked very serious now. "I told you that only you, Bidu, will be able to hear the alarm. When you look at the message, it will be cryptic to everyone but you. Then you can alert your friends. If you are going to another land, most likely they speak a different language there and it won't be English."

"Oh no, I didn't think of that," said Bidu. "What if we have to talk?" She was listening very closely now to every word.

"To communicate with others in another land, you will need to speak in their language. When you want only Piru and Lucinda to understand, you need to speak in English so that no one else knows what you are saying. Gregor knows every language of every land. As long as you have the clock you will automatically be able to speak and understand whatever language is being spoken wherever you are."

"What about Piru and Lucinda? Will they be able to speak and understand as well?"

"Only if they are with you. It's important that you all stay together."

"Wait just a minute," said Bidu's father. "Piru, will fairy dust work back in time? Will you be able to use it?"

"Yes, it will," Piru said sweetly. "It works everywhere, in any land, in any time."

Lucinda wanted to touch the clock too, so she had a question. "Can anyone touch the clock?" she asked Mr. Mayer.

"Gregor can only have one master at a time. So, no, Lucinda, you won't be able to touch the clock. Still, he will be there for all of you, but he will only speak through Bidu."

"Don't worry, Lucinda," said Piru. "You can help with the fairy dust."

Lucinda smiled. That made her happy.

Mr. Mayer had more to say so he just kept on talking. "Gregor can also give you the power of telepathy. Do you know what that means?"

"Maybe you'd better explain it, because I'm not completely sure," said Bidu. Now she looked a little worried.

Mr. Mayer continued. "That means Gregor will be able to communicate with you through the ethers. What he thinks, you will know. And what you think, he will know. So, you can actually have a conversation with Gregor in your mind. You don't need to speak out loud. No one else will be able to hear it. This is for your safety at all times."

Bidu was always thinking of her friends so, of course, she wanted to know if Piru and Lucinda would be telepathic too.

"No," said Mr. Mayer. "When you want to speak with your friends, just speak English and no one else will understand. Gregor can only do telepathy with his master and that will be you, Bidu."

"Oh, one more very important thing," said Mr. Mayer. "As I said before, you girls need to stay together at all times or you will not be able to speak or understand the language. And if you need to return, you must all be in the same space if you call out Gregor's name. You must be as close as you are now to make the journey back safely. Do you understand?"

All three of the girls nodded that they did, indeed, understand.

Bidu smiled at her daddy. "Is it OK, Daddy? Can we go?"

Jim looked at Mr. Mayer. "John, do you think this is a good idea?"

"As long as the girls follow every instruction I have given them, they should be fine. Gregor will assist and guide them. He can do most anything. The most important thing is that the girls stay together."

"What if they should get separated?" Bidu's father wanted to know.

Mr. Mayer paused for a moment and then spoke. "You will have to get back together again or you won't be able to come home. If someone gets lost, the other two of you must find her. This is very important. Gregor will not bring only one or two of you. You must all come back together at the same time."

"We can do this," said Bidu.

Piru and Lucinda were jumping up and down with excitement. Together they were chanting, "We can do this. We can do this. We can do this!"

Jim gave the final nod and Mr. Mayer put the clock in the purple bag. He put the shoulder strap over Bidu's shoulder and opened the bag just enough for the clock face to show.

Piru had one more thing to say. "May I give a little blessing for us before we go?"

"Oh yes, please," said Bidu.

"Yes, please," said Jim.

They all stood close together. Piru removed one of the beads from her necklace. Then they all held hands. Piru began. "Sweet spirits, please be with us. Lead us to where we might be able to do good. Watch over us and keep us safe. Grant us the power of language even if we should get separated. Protect Gregor at all times and watch over Mr. Mayer and our families while we are gone. Amen."

Everyone together said "Amen." With that, Piru sprinkled the fairy dust on herself, Bidu, Lucinda and Gregor. Bidu thought she felt the angels in the room. She looked at Piru, and she could tell by Piru's face that she felt it too. She felt safe.

Mr. Mayer didn't really know what to think about the entire fairy dust incident, but he decided to keep quiet and let the girls have their little fantasy. If it gave them more confidence, then he guessed it couldn't be a bad thing. Besides, he truly believed that anything is possible.

"OK, Mr. Mayer. We're ready. Please help me program Gregor."

They entered the year… backwards. Then they entered TPYGE, which is Egypt backwards.

"You see that little violet light down at the bottom of the clock?"

"Yes," said Bidu.

"When you're ready, just push it."

"Daddy, please tell Mama to hold the chicken and noodles… I bet we'll be so hungry when we get back!"

Jim smiled at his precious daughter and then gave her a big hug and kiss. He also gave hugs to Piru and Lucinda.

"Girls," said Mr. Mayer. "Do you have any other questions before you go?"

"No," said Bidu. "I think we're ready."

"I wish you girls had jackets," Bidu's daddy said. "What if it's cold there?"

"Don't worry," said Piru reassuringly. "I can whip us up jackets or anything else we might need." She started to giggle and then all the girls were giggling.

Mr. Mayer had a puzzled look on his face, but he thought the girls knew more than they were sharing. Jim knew it for sure.

The girls stood close together. Mr. Mayer and Jim went to the other side of the room.

Bidu looked back at her daddy one more time before she pushed the little violet light. He gave her a loving, reassuring look as she set the clock in motion.

The clock began to vibrate as she felt her feet rising up off the floor. Piru and Lucinda were also being raised up. Gregor let off a bunch of white smoke that surrounded the three girls and then in an instant they were gone.

8

Cleopatra

The smoke was clearing and indeed the girls were gone. Jim was having second thoughts about letting his precious daughter go on this adventure. Mr. Mayer could see Jim's apprehension.

"Don't worry, Jim. I have had this clock for years. I have had many conversations with Gregor. I believe there is nothing he can't do to protect and aid those girls. It will be an adventure of a lifetime, for sure. They will have many wonderful stories to tell when they return."

"I'm actually more concerned about how to tell Bidu's mother. I don't think she'll be very happy that I said yes! Will we get any warning as to when the girls might be returning?"

"Actually, no. They will just reappear as they left, including the burst of white smoke. Remember that time travel is not in our time. They may have an adventure that lasts weeks for them, but for us it might only be a day or two. You will barely miss Bidu and it will seem like they are all back before you know it. So, you can tell Marie that they will only be gone a short time."

That made Jim feel a little better. He really did hope the girls had a fun adventure and if truth be known, Jim secretly wished he could have gone too. Maybe next time.

As he walked up the sidewalk in front of his house, he could smell the wonderful aromas coming from their kitchen. He took a deep breath as he thought of just the right words to say to Marie.

****

The girls found themselves on the bank of a river.

"Ooh, I wonder if this is the Nile River?" cried Bidu. "And I wonder where we are in Egypt?"

Right then, Bidu heard an alarm. "Did you girls hear that?" she asked.

"I didn't hear anything," said Piru.

"Me neither," said Lucinda.

The alarm sounded again, just as Bidu figured out it must be Gregor and she was the only one hearing it. She was careful to open the purple bag just like Mr. Mayer showed her. She gently slid the blue door to see if there was a message. The other girls were looking on.

"That doesn't say anything," said Lucinda. "It looks like a bunch of stick people."

Bidu understood it perfectly. It said, "You are in Alexandria. Cleopatra lives in the big palace behind you." Bidu turned around and sure enough there was a huge palace. It looked like the river ran straight to it.

"Maybe we should just follow the river to the palace," she told the girls. Then in her mind she heard, "Bidu. Not so fast. There are many guards and strangers along the way. A storm is coming any minute. You must find safe shelter." It was interesting. When Gregor was speaking in her mind, Bidu couldn't hear a word the girls were saying.

"Bidu, Bidu, what's happening? Why aren't you talking to us?"

Bidu started to laugh. "Girls, do you remember that Gregor will be talking to me in my mind? Well, when he is, I can't hear you. Next time he starts talking, I will hold my hand up so you know. Then you can be quiet until I get the message."

Both girls agreed. It was getting very dark and cold quickly. Bidu could see the clouds getting big and full. They looked ready to explode. She held her hand up to speak to Gregor in her mind. She actually liked this more than reading the messages on the clock.

"Gregor, where can we find shelter?"

"Look to your right. There is a small mud brick house. It is abandoned and vacant. You can find shelter there until the storm passes. You must move quickly before anyone sees you here."

Bidu started moving towards the house waving the girls to follow along.

"I will explain everything, but we must get to that little house right now." As the girls made their way to what looked like a little adobe house, the sky opened up and the rain started to pour down. There was lightning and thunder like they had never heard or seen before. By the time they reached the house, they were all soaked to the bone. The door was covered by a reed mat that Bidu just pushed aside. They went right in. It definitely looked like no one was living there. As Bidu looked around, she saw something that looked like stools. There were some straw beds and carpets on the floor and there was a big trunk with many blankets. She was so happy to see those! They each wrapped themselves in a blanket and tried to warm up. The thunder was so loud that every time it rumbled and boomed, the ground shook. And every crack of lightning lit up the sky like a thousand floodlights. There was a big basket of what looked like dried fruit. Bidu recognized dates and figs. Lucinda and Piru didn't recognize anything, but they were hungry. Bidu offered to taste first to see if they were still edible. They tasted like dried figs and dates to her!

"Come on, girls. Let's eat!"

They each took a big handful and then sat on one of the little stools. They were all happy that there was any food at all. Piru loved the figs best. Lucinda loved it all and so did Bidu. They couldn't believe they could get full on just figs and dates, but they did. They were so grateful that whoever was here before, had left them.

The rain continued to pour as the thunder continued to rumble and roar. The lightning was a bit scary, but beautiful to watch. Bidu wished she would hear from Gregor because she wasn't sure where to go from here. One thing Mr. Mayer hadn't mentioned was how to get in touch with Gregor. She knew he could send her an alarm, but she wasn't sure how to contact him herself. She discussed this dilemma with the girls.

Lucinda had the first suggestion.

"Maybe there is a button on the clock that calls him."

Piru thought a minute and said, "Why not just call his name… but only once. We don't want to go back home yet!"

Bidu looked at the clock for a new button but didn't see anything that Mr. Mayer hadn't already told her about. She liked Piru's suggestion so she opened the bag and gently lifted Gregor to the edge of the opening.

She called to him. "Gregor?" And then she waited. She didn't want to say his name again.

Nothing happened. Then she decided to try calling him in her mind. "Gregor, please talk to me," she thought.

"Hello, Bidu. How may I serve you?"

"Oh, Gregor, I'm so happy to hear from you. So you mean that whenever I want to talk to you, I can?"

"Yes, Bidu. Just think my name, and I'll respond. I don't respond to you saying my name out loud. That is for your safety. You wouldn't want anyone to hear you and discover the clock. So calling out my name is only for when you want to go home."

"OK," said Bidu. "I understand." She was still learning more about Gregor. She sent him a thought. "Is there anything I can do for you, Gregor?"

"Yes, Bidu. Keep me safe and be aware of everything around you."

"Oh yes, I will keep you safe and I will take care of you. Can you always tell if there is danger?"

"Yes, Bidu. I can feel it. And when I do, I will let you know. I will guide you every way I can, but you can never tell anyone or let on that you have me in your possession."

"I understand," said Bidu again. And she did. In fact, she decided to put the purple bag under her shirt so that it didn't show to anyone. Then she told the girls never to talk about the clock to anyone. Both Piru and Lucinda knew how important this was and they agreed.

The rain was easing up and the thunder and lightning had stopped. It was very dark.

"Let's try to get some sleep," Bidu said. "There are plenty of blankets." They all wrapped themselves up and cuddled together to stay warm. They seemed happy for their adventure, and no one seemed to feel any danger… except Gregor.

****

It was morning. The storm had passed and the sun was coming up. The girls were awakened by the light of day. They were all excited about going to meet Cleopatra. Gregor listened to them for a while as they talked about following the river to the palace. Then he sent an alarm to Bidu. She recognized the sound right away this time. The girls didn't bother to look on to see the message, because they couldn't read it anyway.

But Bidu could. It said, "Don't do anything just yet. Stay in the house. The soldiers are out doing their morning patrol."

While Bidu was reading the message, Piru had gone to the front of the house. She lifted the reed mat covering the door.

"Oh, look how beautiful it is out there. So many horses. Maybe we can go for a ride."

Bidu shouted at Piru, "Move away from the door. Those are soldiers and we don't want to be seen."

But it was too late. One of the soldiers saw and heard Piru. He came closer for another look. Piru rushed back into the house. Bidu put Gregor back into her shirt just as the soldier came into the house.

"And what have we here?" he said. "Three little girls looking for trouble?"

"Oh no, sir," said Bidu, trying to calm him down. "We are just traveling to see some relatives."

"What is this little girl with the yellow hair? We don't have yellow-haired children here. In fact, I have never seen a child with yellow hair. I think you will have to come with me."

"Run, Piru, run!" yelled Bidu.

Piru ran around the soldier and out the door, but she still wasn't used to her human legs. They were still a bit wobbly. She tripped and the soldier laughed as he picked her up to put her on the big white horse he was riding.

Bidu was screaming in her mind. "Gregor, what do I do? We can't lose Piru."

"First stay calm," Gregor instructed. "You will not be able to get Piru back. But you can go with her. If you go outside, there will be many more soldiers. They will probably take you and Lucinda too if you go out and start running. It's the only way you can see where Piru is being taken. Hurry!"

Bidu didn't think about it. She just told Lucinda to run out the door with her. She was scared, but she had to protect Piru. The girls ran outside and ran in the direction Piru was heading. They could hear Piru yelling for Bidu. Bidu had big tears in her eyes. She knew how sweet and innocent Piru was. She didn't have a mean bone in her human body... or her fairy body, for that matter. She was all goodness.

There were about 15 more soldiers all on horses. When they saw the girls running around, the boss started laughing.

"Go and pick those crazy children up. Take them to the palace dungeon until we decide what to do with them."

The soldiers charged at the girls. One of them rode right up alongside Bidu and swooped her up onto his horse. The soldiers were all laughing and riding in circles like this was some kind of fun game for them.

Then another soldier, rode up alongside Lucinda, who was crying and running at the same time. He bent down, pulling her up onto his horse. The girls had no idea where they were going but they knew they were at the mercy of these soldiers.

"Gregor, please talk to me!" cried Bidu in her mind.

"Stay calm. Tell the other girls to stay calm. You will now have to go to the palace. Do what they tell you to do. They can be very mean if you try to defy them in any way. You are children, so they will not harm you."

Lucinda was riding on a horse that was right next to Bidu, so Bidu tried to calm her by telling her it would be OK, but she could see how scared Lucinda was. Piru was way up ahead and Bidu couldn't get close enough to talk to her, but she could see her. It looked like they were all being taken to the same place. The soldiers rode down by the river. The scenery to the palace was beautiful but the girls didn't really notice. The palace got bigger and bigger as they got closer. When they arrived at the huge front bridge, someone lowered it so that all the soldiers and horses could cross.

Gregor sent a message in his mind to Bidu.

"Try not to speak English to the girls right now. You don't want to make the soldiers suspicious of you. Wait until you are inside the palace and more alone."

Bidu thanked Gregor. Lucinda tried to say something in English and Bidu immediately put her finger to her lips to signal her to be quiet. Lucinda understood and stopped trying to communicate. Bidu smiled at her to try to reassure her. Lucinda tried to give a little smile back, but inside she was really scared.

As the soldiers were all waiting for the bridge to be lowered, Bidu got closer to Piru. She signaled her to be quiet too, and Piru understood. Their eyes met, and Piru felt better that Bidu was there. Once the bridge was lowered, all of the soldiers rode into the big plaza area. The boss began to give the orders. Bidu and the girls understood the language they were speaking.

"Take these children down to the dungeon. Put them in the holding cell until I can talk to Cleopatra to find out what is to be done with them. Don't hurt them. You know how she feels about children."

All of the soldiers replied, "Yes, sir!" in unison. The girls did breathe a little sigh of relief that the boss had told them not to hurt the girls. Bidu was hoping they would be together so they could talk, but for now they only looked at each other.

They rode down a very winding road that went underneath the palace. It was cold and damp there. The three soldiers carrying the girls, went all the way down while the other soldiers took their horses to the stables. The soldiers did not speak to the girls. When they got down to the dungeon, the soldiers pulled the girls off their horses and carried them to a big dark cell.

They put the three girls inside and locked the big iron door. There was only one bench and all the girls sat right next to each other. One of the soldiers said, "Wait here," in their language. All the girls nodded. They understood and they were grateful for that.

Once the soldiers were out of sight and the girls were alone, Bidu took Piru's and Lucinda's hands in hers.

"Don't worry, girls. I just know we're going to be OK." Bidu tried to sound very convincing, but deep down, she was scared too. She held her hand up because she needed to talk to Gregor in her mind. She had no idea what to do now.

"Gregor, now what?" she asked.

"At some point, the soldiers will come for you again. They will take you to the palace."

Bidu didn't know what to say. She had so many questions.

Gregor continued. "You will probably have an audience with Cleopatra at some point. Bidu, you must be listening for me in your mind so that I can talk to you while you are inside the palace but I will try only to talk to you when you can listen to me. When Cleopatra is speaking, you need to only listen to her. If you are distracted in any way, she will see that and think you are being rude and disrespectful. She is favorable towards children, but she is very hard on anyone who disrespects her. For your first meeting, just listen and only speak if she asks you a question.

"OK," said Bidu.

"And you do the talking unless Cleopatra asks a question directly to one of the other girls."

"What if she asks where we are from?" Bidu wanted to know.

"I think it's best to be honest with her," replied Gregor. "She will be able to tell if you are making up stories."

"Yes, but our story sounds made up," Bidu answered.

"I don't think you should lie about visiting relatives. You don't know your way around Alexandria and you would not be able to answer any questions. I do know that Cleopatra is fascinated by wizardry and magic so if you are genuine and honest about where you came from, I think she might listen. But never, never tell about the clock… no matter what."

Bidu relayed the message to the other girls who understood.

Just then, two guards came towards the cold cell. One of them had a big set of keys. One of the keys opened the big iron door to the cell they were in. The guards didn't speak, they just signaled for the girls to follow them. One led the way, the other stayed behind the girls to watch them. They walked up what seemed like a thousand steps in the winding stairway. When they got to the top and the doors opened, the girls couldn't believe their eyes.

The palace was huge with a big marble floor and very high walls, also marble. There were giant vases filled with all kinds of colorful flowers. There were lots of attendants cleaning and dusting. They walked through the big foyer into another large room. Right at the end of the room was a huge throne with two big red velvet chairs and four smaller chairs. Sitting in one of the big chairs was a beautiful woman. She had thick black hair and a long powder-blue robe. She was wearing a crown full of all kinds of colorful jewels. She had a kind look on her face, but she was not smiling. She raised her hand to signal to the girls to come forward.

One of the guards said, "You must curtsy to the Queen."

The girls stepped forward and did their best to comply.

Cleopatra spoke. "You may rise. I'm told you were found outside the palace. What were you doing there?"

Bidu took one step forward. "We were hoping to see the palace."

"Well now you are in the palace. And that means that now you can serve me."

Bidu looked up at Cleopatra. "It would be our honor."

Now, Bidu didn't understand one word of what she was saying, but the words seemed to just come as Gregor had promised.

Cleopatra looked at the girls. "You look like decent children. I must admit I have never seen a child with yellow hair. The only one of you that really looks like us is you." She pointed to Lucinda. Lucinda's hair looked like Cleopatra's. Lucinda did another curtsy.

Cleopatra continued. "We have a children's area and I have two small children who spend most of their days there. They need to learn things and also be entertained. I had to let the last attendants for the children go because they couldn't seem to keep the children happy and it's very important that the children are happy."

"Guards, take these girls to the children's area. Get them some proper attendants clothing and have them meet the children. You will report back to me at the end of the day and then we will see what is going to happen with them. Now, take them away."

All three girls did one more curtsy. Bidu was glad that Cleopatra hadn't asked more questions. They followed the guards to the dressing room where they were given white robes to wear over their clothing. Bidu still had Gregor under her shirt and the robe actually disguised the clock very well. Once they were dressed in their robes, they were taken to the children's area which looked like its own mini palace. There were two children as Cleopatra had said. The girl was being chased by the boy who was very loud and unruly. The girl seemed like she was very frustrated with him. When they saw the three girls they both went over to them.

"What are your names?" asked the girl.

"I'm Bidu, this is Piru, and this is Lucinda. What are your names?"

The boy answered first. "I'm Caesarion (*See-zar-ee-un*) and this is my sister, Cleopatra Selene, but we all call her Selene (*Sell-eene*)."

"Those are lovely names," said Bidu.

With that, Caesarion started pushing his sister and tugging at her robe. "Chase me," he said. "Come on, chase me."

"I don't feel like it," Selene said trying to get away from him.

Caesarion started to yell and throw a big tantrum. He got into everything, threw everything and had no regard for his sister or any of the girls. He was probably the worst behaved little boy that Bidu had ever seen. Piru hadn't spent much time with human children other than Bidu, so she just couldn't believe what she was seeing! Lucinda was bothered by it all too, but she had no idea how to control him.

Bidu looked at the other girls and wasn't sure just what to do. Thank goodness that the attendants brought in lunch. It had been a very troubled morning, but maybe lunch would calm him down. Besides, the girls were starving and couldn't wait to eat too! In came a big, beautiful tray of all kinds of wonderful foods. Some Bidu didn't recognize, but she decided to try everything. First, she made plates for Caesarion and Selene. They sat at a little table. Bidu, Piru, and Lucinda filled their plates and sat down to enjoy a wonderful lunch, but Caesarion had other plans. He threw food and grabbed food off everyone's plate. He had absolutely no manners. The girls finally stood up and held their plates above Caesarion's head. He, of course, threw a big fit, but Lucinda couldn't help herself and she started to laugh. They did the best they could to finish lunch. Once everyone seemed to have had enough to eat, Bidu shrugged her shoulders at the girls and said, "Now what?" No one seemed to know what to do.

Gregor could sense Bidu's uncertainty. He called to her.

"Bidu, you need to take control here. You know lots of games from the future that these children do not know. Caesarion will be a real challenge, so try to pick a game he would like first."

Bidu spoke softly to the other girls about choosing a game while the children were still running around like wild animals. Well, actually it was more like Caesarion running after his sister and she was just running to get away from him.

As the girls looked around the room, they saw what looked like round balls, but they were not made of rubber and they didn't bounce. Instead, they were made of papyrus paper and animal skins. The balls gave Bidu the idea of Hot Potato. Trying to get Caesarion to calm down took a very long time. Selene just waited and kept asking all kinds of questions of the girls. It seemed like the more they all tried to ignore Caesarion, the louder he got.

"Hey, Caesarion," said Bidu, "I have a fun new game for you! Would you like to play?" she said as she picked up one of the balls.

Caesarion grabbed the ball from Bidu and threw it at Lucinda. He laughed and laughed.

No one else laughed.

Bidu got everyone to sit in a circle. Everyone except Caesarion that is. Once all the girls were starting to play and have fun, then Caesarion began to notice. He came over to where the girls were.

"I want to play," he demanded.

"OK," said Bidu. "Sit down and I'll explain everything."

She showed them how to sit in the circle and how to roll the ball while barely touching it, pretending it was a hot potato.

Caesarion seemed to like the game, but he would push the ball so hard that it hurt his sister.

Bidu signaled to Piru and they stepped aside to talk in English. Bidu asked, "What do you think of using a little…"

Piru knew exactly what Bidu was thinking.

"Fairy dust?" she asked.

"Exactly," replied Bidu.

"Great idea," said Piru. "We'll help him be the sweetest boy in all of Alexandria!"

"Let's make a game out of it," said Piru. "Bidu, why don't you tell them a story about fairies and see if you can get Caesarion to close his eyes at some point. Lucinda, you can sprinkle the dust and I'll be the voice of the fairy."

Bidu was all out of ideas, so this sounded like it just might work.

"OK, you two," she said to the children. "Gather around. I will tell you an amazing story of magic." She was so surprised when Caesarion ran up to her and sat right down.

"Oh, I love magic!" he said.

"Great!" said Bidu. "Then you will love this!" Bidu began her story. She actually told the true story of how she found a real fairy and helped mend her wing so she could take her back to her land. Caesarion was mesmerized by this story. When she got to the part about making fairy dust, he wanted to know more.

Bidu said, "Why don't we just show you what fairy dust can do?"

Caesarion loved that idea. Selene loved it too.

Bidu continued. "Close your eyes. Listen to the voice of the fairy as she casts a spell on you and then you must keep your eyes closed. You will feel the fairy dust fall on you. You must not open your eyes or the spell will be broken."

Finally, Caesarion was paying attention. "Can I make a wish?" he asked.

Bidu had to think fast. She had no idea what kind of wish he would make and if it could even be granted.

Piru jumped in. "Fairies can only cast spells. They can't grant wishes. And they can only cast good spells. I promise you will love it."

Caesarion wasn't sure about that. He really wanted to become magic, but he decided that it was interesting enough to sit a little longer.

Lucinda was happy to participate too, so she told them a little about the battle and how the fairy dust changed everyone in the land so that they were all happy together. Selene loved that story, but Caesarion was more interested in what it would do for him.

There were two little cots in the children's room. Bidu asked the children to go to lie down as the spell was cast. She told them that they could not speak or open their eyes until the fairy voice told them to. They practically ran to the cots. They were really excited! Once they were settled down and their eyes were closed, Bidu reminded them not to open their eyes or the spell would be broken. They both had their eyes shut tight. Then Bidu nodded to Piru to cast the spell.

She began speaking softly. "Sweet spirits, we need a special spell to be cast on Selene and Caesarion. They will be showered with fairy dust and they will feel joy and happiness instantly when they feel the fairy dust fall on their skin. They will feel this same joy and happiness every day. They will share their joy and happiness with everyone. The more they share, the more joyful and happy they will be. They will feel love for everyone and everything. This spell will be forever cast. It cannot ever be broken. And so it is."

With the last words of the spell, Bidu took one of her beads and handed it to Lucinda who opened it and sprinkled it onto both of the children. The girls were happy when they heard the angels sing.

"OK," said Piru. "Now you can open your eyes, but don't get up too soon. Just sit for a minute and tell me how you feel."

"I feel happy," said Selene.

"I feel happy too," said Caesarion. Then he leaned over and gave Selene a big hug. She couldn't believe it. But it sure felt good. The rest of the afternoon went smoothly and lovingly. The girls taught the children a lot of games from the future, including Simon Says, and Hopscotch. And finally Caesarion could sit still long enough to learn some songs from the future too. He really loved Itsy Bitsy Spider. Selene's favorite was Twinkle, Twinkle Little Star. They both seemed fascinated with stories from all of the girls about their adventures and what life was like in the future.

About three o'clock, Cleopatra entered the room. The children were having a great time. When they saw their mother, they both ran over to her with big hugs.

"Hi, Mommy," said Caesarion as he wrapped his arms around Cleopatra's legs and held on tight. Cleopatra looked at Bidu with much surprise.

"My, my!" she exclaimed. "Whatever happened to my little boy? I can't remember the last time he came to hug me. This is wonderful!"

Then it was Selene's turn to give her mother a big, long hug. The joy could be felt by everyone in the room.

"We will have our family dinner tonight at 6:00 pm," Cleopatra announced. "I would like you three girls to join us."

"Oh goody," squealed Caesarion as he jumped up and down and clapped his hands. Selene was happy too.

"Why don't you children come with me and let these girls have a rest before dinner? You girls can freshen up and relax in the attendant room over there through that door. We will see you at dinner."

All three girls did a big curtsy for Cleopatra. Both of her children took one of their mother's hands. She looked back at the girls and smiled. Then she left the room with her two happy, joyful, loving and very different children.

The girls went into the attendant room. It felt good to just sit down and relax. They were talking about the day and how amazing it was that they were actually inside Cleopatra's palace. Earlier, they were all so scared when the soldiers had captured them, and even worse, they had to deal with children that were never taught how to behave. They laughed about how they got the children to lie down long enough to have a spell cast on them. They could tell that Cleopatra saw the difference in her children and they thought she was happy about it. They settled into just having a nice quiet rest for a while. All was calm when Bidu got the alarm from Gregor. She checked the clock to see that Gregor was letting her know danger was coming.

All of a sudden there was a pounding on the door. Four big guards burst in with chains. They were yelling commands.

"Don't move!"

"Hold your hands behind your back!"

"Don't try anything funny!"

The girls didn't know what was happening. They were put in chains and dragged away by the mean guards. They were taken back to the dungeon, into that cold damp cell. They just didn't understand what was happening. Bidu tried to talk to one of the guards.

"Shut up!" yelled the guard. "We don't want to hear anything you have to say."

The chains were removed as the girls were thrown into the cell. Piru fell down and skinned her knee. It started to bleed. Piru was such a gentle soul. She just couldn't believe they could be so mean. What was worse was that she had no idea why. She wondered if it was her yellow hair.

Lucinda lay quietly on the floor as the tears rolled down her cheeks. She wanted to go home.

Bidu was thrown against the wall and slid down to the floor. Her shoulder was hurt but she couldn't think about that right now. She felt responsible for her friends, but didn't know what to do. She thought Cleopatra was happy with how wonderful the children were now. She thought they were doing something for good. She wanted to call out to Gregor, but she heard the guards coming back.

"Get up!" they yelled. "Cleopatra wants to see you. NOW!"

The girls were put in chains again and dragged away.

9

Back to the Future

The doors to the big dining room were thrown open by the guards.

"Here they are, Your Highness," said the head guard, as he shoved the girls into the room. Cleopatra's face turned bright red as her voice exploded out of her mouth.

"What are those girls doing in chains?" she yelled. "Remove those chains at once!"

"But you said to bring the girls to you right away. I thought you were angry with them."

"You imbeciles!" shouted Cleopatra. "I never said to put them in chains or to lock them up. And look, Piru is bleeding."

She called to her attendant, "Call the doctor immediately."

She looked at all of the girls apologetically. "I'm so sorry, girls. I never meant for this to happen. I wanted you to have dinner with us so that I could thank you for all you have done for my children. Please accept my apologies for this."

Then she directed her attention to the guards. "You four idiots will spend the night in chains in the dungeon yourselves. And there will be no dinner for any of you. I will decide tomorrow what your punishment will be for this outrage."

"Please, Your Highness," said the biggest guard. "We're sorry for the misunderstanding."

"Misunderstanding?" screamed Cleopatra. "This is the most idiotic thing you have ever done. These girls are my guests and they are to be treated as such at all times."

"Yes, Your Highness," said the guard. "Please give us another chance."

"Another chance?" Cleopatra yelled. "Why you'll be lucky if you get to keep your stupid heads."

She clapped her hands for the two guards who were standing by the doors to come closer. She pointed to the guards who had made a terrible mistake.

"Take them to the dungeon. Chain them and leave them. Tomorrow they will be back to shoveling horse poop again."

"Yes, Your Highness," they said as they chained the other guards and took them away.

The girls didn't know what to do. They were still shaken up from being thrown into the dungeon. They all just stood quietly waiting. Cleopatra walked over to them. She waved for the children to come over. Caesarion was there first with a big hug, followed by Selene.

"Are you OK?" Caesarion asked Bidu. Selene was trying to comfort Piru and Lucinda, who was still crying a little.

Cleopatra took Lucinda's face in her hands and looked into her eyes.

"I'm so sorry, my dear. Those guards have been stable guards taking care of horses. They just got promoted to being inside this palace. I may have made a terrible mistake thinking that they were ready to be in charge, inside. They will not be allowed in here again. Let's get you all cleaned up and then we will have a wonderful feast."

All of the girls were happy that this ordeal was not going to be one of dungeons and chains, but they were still recovering from the shock of it all.

The doctor came into the dining room with a little black bag of potions and creams. He went to Piru first because her knee was still bleeding. He washed the area and then put a special cream on it. The cream burned, but Piru tried to be brave. She held back her tears. She really wanted her mother at this moment, but that was not possible so she looked at Bidu.

Bidu looked back with her loving and understanding eyes. That made Piru feel better.

Lucinda wasn't really hurt, just scared and sad. The doctor looked her over, then asked Selene to take Lucinda and Piru to the girls' powder room so they could wash their hands and faces.

Then the doctor turned to Bidu. Her face and hands needed washing too, but he had a feeling that he saw pain in her face.

"Does anything hurt you?" he asked.

"Well," said Bidu, "I think I hurt my shoulder when I hit the wall in the dungeon."

"Let's have a look at that," the doctor said. He began to slowly move Bidu's arm, but when he lifted it up, Bidu winced in pain.

"I think you have a shoulder sprain," the doctor told her.

"Let's put a sling on your arm to hold it in place. If you can keep it as still as possible for a few days, I think it will feel much better. In the meantime, put this cream on it twice a day and it will help it heal."

"OK," said Bidu. She thought the cream smelled like dirt, but she let the doctor put it on her anyway. And the sling did help her to not move her arm. Bidu was so happy that the doctor never noticed the clock tucked away under her robe.

"Can I go to wash too?" she asked. She really wanted to see her friends.

"Of course," he said with a smile. "I'll take you. It's on the way back to the infirmary."

The other girls were washing up but they were so happy to see Bidu. They waited for her to get cleaned up and then Selene took them all back to the dining room.

When they walked into the dining room this time, there was music playing. It was happy music. There were some girls and boys dancing while others were playing musical instruments. Cleopatra got up to meet them herself and then escorted them to special seats at the front of the room where she sat.

"Tonight, you are the special guests of the palace," she said.

The girls smiled. They still couldn't believe how this had happened after they were viciously captured by the guards, but they were glad to be guests of Cleopatra.

"Tonight, this dinner is for you, girls. You have made my children so happy. I want to honor you all. Special foods have been prepared for you. First, we will dine and enjoy the entertainment, and then I want to talk with you to get to know you better. The children have told me of so many things that I have never heard of before. I am anxious to know many things about you and where you have come from."

Bidu shot a glance to Piru, then to Lucinda. They each seemed to know what the others were thinking.

Oh, how she wished she could talk to Gregor. Somehow, she would have to get away to talk with him. She was nervous about what to say and how to answer Cleopatra's questions. But for now, she decided it would be best to try to enjoy the dinner and the entertainment.

Gregor could feel Bidu's apprehension. He thought it best to try to communicate with her to reassure her. "Bidu, this is Gregor."

Bidu sat up and tried not to look startled. Of course, she could only talk to him in her mind.

"Oh, Gregor. I'm so glad to hear from you. I'm so confused. I don't know what to say to Cleopatra about where we are from and…"

Gregor interrupted her. "Bidu, take a deep breath. This will all work out. Cleopatra loves you and what you have done for her children. They told her of the games you taught them and of the stories you told them. Of course, she wants to know more about what you are telling her children. And she loves stories of magic and fantasy, so it stands to reason that she would want to know more."

"But what should I say? How much should I tell her?" Bidu asked.

"I think you should tell her the truth," Gregor advised.

"But you said never to tell about you."

"Yes, I did. You can never, ever tell her about me or the clock. There would be people who would want to take me and use me for their selfish desires."

Bidu tried to hold back her tears. "Then what do you mean 'tell the truth'? I don't understand."

"Bidu, I mean to tell her you have come from the future."

"But what if she asks me how I came to be here?"

"That's a great question," said Gregor.

Just then Bidu heard Cleopatra's voice. "Are you alright, Bidu? You look like you just saw a snake."

Gregor spoke to Bidu. "Excuse yourself and go to the bathroom."

"I'm so sorry, Cleopatra," Bidu explained. "I think I'm still upset by what happened earlier. May I please excuse myself to go to the powder room? I think I just need a moment."

"Of course," said Cleopatra trying to be understanding.

"Would you like me to send an attendant with you?"

"Oh no, thank you," said Bidu. "I think I just need a minute alone. I won't be long."

"All right," said Cleopatra. "We will wait to serve the dinner until you return."

"Thank you so much." With that, Bidu got up and left the table. She tried to glance at Piru and Lucinda to reassure them. Piru thought she understood exactly what was going on. She touched Lucinda's hand to signal to her that all was well. That seemed to satisfy her.

Once Bidu was safely alone in the powder room, she called to Gregor. "Please talk to me. I'm alone now."

"You must listen carefully, Bidu. Try not to interrupt and let me explain everything."

Bidu was quiet as Gregor went on. "Cleopatra will want to know where you come from. Tell her that this story might seem crazy, but that you came from the future. Tell her it's 2000 years in the future. You ended up here because a wizard put a spell on you girls for trespassing and sent you 2000 years back in time. You had no idea where you would end up until you got here. The only reason you recognize this place is because you studied it in school. Right now, you have no idea how to get back home. Do you understand all of this?"

"Yes, Gregor, but won't she ask more questions?"

"Of course, she will be very curious about the future and she will want to know all about it. She consults with fortune tellers and is fascinated with knowing what is ahead. Be sure you stress that you have no idea how to get back. Do not act like you have any special powers at all. Do offer to answer any and all of her questions about what's coming in the future as best you can. Since you are only 11 years old, she won't expect you to know everything. You can always say you don't know about everything she is asking about. Tell her stories about things you have in the future that do not exist here, like television, computers and even microwaves. She will be so fascinated, she will never want you to leave."

"Oh, Gregor, I think I can do this, but what about the fairy dust and Piru being a fairy?"

"I wouldn't mention that right away. Just act as though you three are friends from the future. We can talk later about whether or not to tell about fairies. That might be too much for her to know right now. Keep things simple. You have enough to talk about and share with her to keep her interested without bringing fairies and fairy dust into this."

"What if she asks about how Caesarion changed so much and what if he told her of the fairy dust."

"Bidu, you are over thinking everything. You can always tell her you made up a story to get him to behave and he believed it. She will believe that because she is fascinated by mind power and magic. Just don't tell her you can do magic or she will have all kinds of assignments for you. Remember you are just three girls who got caught on someone else's property and, unfortunately for you, he was a wizard who put a spell on you. It's really not that complicated, and I will be with you through everything. If you don't have any questions, then go back to the dinner and try to enjoy the celebration. Don't forget to breathe. You've got this, Bidu!"

Bidu took a few deep breaths, then walked back to the dining room. She patted her purple bag and wondered if Gregor could feel it. She felt lots better now. She decided to make a game out of this. She would try to keep Cleopatra entertained with her amazing stories. After all, her father always told her how active her imagination was. Now might be a good time to use it!

Bidu walked back into the dining room. Both Piru and Lucinda ran up to her.

"Are you OK?" asked Piru and Lucinda at the same time.

"Yes, girls," said Bidu smiling at her friends. She looked over at Cleopatra, and saw Cleopatra smile at her. She smiled back to let her know that all was well. Cleopatra clapped her hands together three times. The attendants began to bring in huge platters of all kinds of wonderful foods. The music began to play again, and it felt like a big festive party. Caesarion and Selene wanted to sit next to the girls, so they all had to rearrange the seating, but it didn't take long for everyone to be settled and happy. Big trays of fish and fowl were passed around first, then a huge platter of all kinds of colorful vegetables. The aromas of the food were wonderful and everything tasted so delicious.

The girls really liked the bread that was baked with honey and dates. Then out came a big bowl of something Bidu had never seen before. If she had never had it, then she was sure that Piru and Lucinda hadn't ever seen it before either. Bidu leaned over and asked Selene if she knew what it was. Selene laughed.

"Of course, silly," she giggled. "It's lentils. They are delicious. Try them."

None of the girls had ever heard of lentils, but they didn't want to hurt Cleopatra's feelings because it seemed that this was a very special dish in their land.

First, Bidu took a spoonful. She rolled it around in her mouth letting the flavors bathe her tongue. She decided that she really liked it. Then Piru, who was still getting used to human food, took a bite. She wasn't sure what to think, but as she tasted it, she smiled and then took another bite. That made Lucinda ready to try it too. And she loved it! She had two big helpings. Bidu couldn't wait to get home to tell her mother about lentils. She would have to get the recipe from Cleopatra. While Bidu was thinking of her mother, she started to feel homesick. She did miss her family, and she knew the other girls were also missing home too. She was glad that they were all here together. She didn't want to focus on feeling homesick, so she tried to stay in the moment of this amazing feast. She wanted to remember every detail of it so that she would never forget this experience.

Everyone was eating and talking and laughing. The music was playing again as the dancers came out to put on a spectacular show. The girls loved the costumes and it was easy to see that everyone was having a wonderful time. Cleopatra glanced over at Bidu and the girls many times to make sure they were enjoying themselves. She was happy because it was obvious that they were!

The feast went on for hours until Cleopatra was ready for it to end. She clapped her hands for the attendants to begin cleaning up.

Cleopatra walked over to the girls, told the children to kiss the girls goodnight, then asked them to follow her to her personal reception room. Bidu started to feel a little nervous, because even though Gregor had told her what to say, she was hoping that Cleopatra wouldn't ask her a question that she couldn't answer. She touched Gregor and felt better. She thought of how her mother always told her she was divinely protected and that everything was just the way it was supposed to be. That made her feel better too.

The girls followed Cleopatra to the most amazing room. It had all white marble walls and floors. There were big, beautiful fountains with water running from the fountains into a huge pool. There were big blue lounge chairs set up all around. On one of the lounges sat two cats. They had collars with jewels and they looked very regal. Bidu loved cats, so she noticed them right away.

"Oh, Cleopatra, I didn't know you would have cats here. They are one of my favorite animals!" Bidu exclaimed.

Cleopatra seemed amused. "Cats are very special animals in Egypt. We believe that they are magical creatures and they bring us good luck. We treat them like royalty."

"What are their names?" asked Bidu.

"The white one is named Rana. The brown one is named Nada."

"Can we pet them?" Bidu asked.

"Of course," said Cleopatra. "They are very friendly. Come and sit down and the cats will come to you."

Cleopatra signaled to the girls to sit all together. As soon as they sat down, Rana and Nada came right up to them. Oh how they loved being petted by the girls. Both of the cats were purring as they nuzzled each of them.

Cleopatra sat on a lounge that faced all three of the girls. She let them pet the cats for a while; then she began speaking.

"So, where do you girls come from?"

Bidu took a deep breath. "I know this might sound a little crazy, but we actually come from the future. Two thousand years in the future."

Bidu thought that alone would be enough to shock Cleopatra, but it didn't. Cleopatra looked at Bidu waiting for more.

Bidu went on to tell Cleopatra of how they were trespassing and how a wizard had cast a spell on them sending them back in time. Cleopatra wasn't sure what to believe, but the more Bidu told her of her life in the future, the more she believed it. Of course, she wanted to hear everything and she had one question after another. She wanted to know about politics, and religion, and wizards casting spells. She wanted to know what the schoolbooks said about her and Egypt. She wanted Bidu to tell her future to her along with all that was going to happen. Bidu did her best to answer every question but she did not tell of the future for Cleopatra. In fact, she did not tell of anything that might make Cleopatra feel bad.

"Why can't you tell me my future?" Cleopatra asked.

"I'm so sorry," said Bidu, "but I am only in sixth grade and we have not yet studied world history, so I'm afraid I can't tell you anything. The only thing I remember about history is that the country I come from, America, wasn't even discovered until almost fifteen hundred years from now."

Cleopatra seemed amazed that there were more lands in the world. She really wanted to know more about what Bidu knew about Egypt, but she actually believed her story about not knowing world history just yet. It was hard to believe that these girls were only 11 years old. They seemed way more mature than that.

Cleopatra wanted to know everything from what food they ate, to what kind of clothes they wore. She wanted to know all about the games they played, and the books they read. She loved hearing about airplanes and cars but she could barely comprehend it because, for them, transportation was horses and chariots. The thought of something flying through the sky, other than a bird, seemed like a fairy tale.

She could see that Bidu and the girls were getting tired, but she didn't want to stop. It was after midnight and the girls began yawning, so finally, Cleopatra suggested they all go to the bath house for a bath. They could talk more tomorrow. Bidu had no idea what more she could tell Cleopatra, but she knew there would be endless questions.

The girls were so happy to be done... at least for a while. Bidu's throat was dry from talking so much. Cleopatra escorted them to the most amazing bath house. More white marble with huge tubs of warm water. The girls all had special bathing suits laid out for them by the attendants.

"You will be well taken care of by my special attendants. Please enjoy your baths. There are pitchers of tea and juices for you to enjoy. Have a good night's sleep and I will see you all in the morning."

The girls were happy to have Cleopatra leave them alone. Bidu could see that Piru and Lucinda had a lot to say, but she signaled them to be quiet. She didn't want any of the attendants to tell Cleopatra of anything they were saying. Bidu was careful to secretly slip the purple bag off her shoulder and tuck it under one of the towels on her lounge chair. Once the girls slipped into the warm and wonderful water, one of the attendants told them, "Please ring the bell if you need anything, or when you are ready to get out of the tub. We will be right here to attend to you." Then they left the room.

The three girls enjoyed their baths. And this gave them an opportunity to talk to each other.

"Oh my," said Piru. "I thought Cleopatra would talk all night!"

"Yes," agreed Lucinda. "Bidu, you handled everything just right. I love the story about the wizard. It sounded so real."

"Thank goodness for Gregor. He told me what to say. I was nervous, but I think Cleopatra is satisfied with what I told her."

The girls all agreed that it had gone well and they felt pretty safe.

When they were ready to get out of the bath, there were new, clean robes waiting for them along with wonderful fragrant lotions for them to rub onto their skin.

Bidu couldn't wait to put Gregor back over her shoulder. She felt safe when she could feel him near. When they were dressed again and ready, they rang the bell for the attendants. They came right away and escorted them to their room in the attendant area. The three girls had their own room together, and they were very happy to see that!

Once the attendants had left them, they closed the door and sat on their beds. Piru spoke first.

"Bidu, how long do we have to stay here? I miss my family so much."

Lucinda agreed as tears filled her eyes.

"I understand," said Bidu. "I promise you, we will leave soon. I just have to figure out how to make this all happen."

"Why can't we just have Gregor take us home now?" Piru asked.

"Yes," said Lucinda.

"We could be gone in the morning and they will never know."

"I hear you girls," said Bidu with compassion. "But for some reason, I'm thinking we need to stay just a little while longer and say a proper goodbye."

"What does that mean?" said Piru. "Why can't we just leave a note and go? Cleopatra will never want us to leave."

Bidu did understand how the girls were feeling and she too wanted to go home, but she didn't want to insult Cleopatra.

"Let me think about this, girls."

Just then, the doors to her room burst open. It was Cleopatra.

"Is Caesarion here with you girls?" she asked frantically.

"No," said Bidu. "Why, is something wrong?"

"He's missing!" cried Cleopatra. "And I've just been informed that the guards from the stables escaped from their cells. They were angry with me. If you see or hear anything please let me know."

Bidu thought she saw tears in Cleopatra's eyes. Once Cleopatra was gone, Piru spoke up.

"Bidu, those guards were so mean. They might blame us too for being thrown into the dungeon. Please let's go home. I'm so scared."

"I think we should try to help find Caesarion," said Bidu. "Maybe they just took him to the dungeon."

"I don't want to go back to the dungeon," cried Piru. "I just want to go home."

Bidu thought for a moment. "OK, Piru. I know how you feel. Give me a few minutes to go to the dungeon and see if I can help find Caesarion. You girls stay here, and I will come back."

"No Bidu," said Lucinda. "What if they capture you? Then we can never get back."

Bidu stopped. "You may be right, Lucinda. Piru, I think you should change me into a fairy. That way I can go undetected. Let me see what I can see down there."

"I'm so afraid, Bidu. Maybe I could make you into a very small fairy, smaller than a fly even. Then you could go to look, but you wouldn't be able to do anything other than look when you're that small."

"I think that is a good idea," said Bidu. "Give me one minute."

Then she called to Gregor to make sure he could be part of the spell. She didn't want to leave him behind while she went on this mission. Gregor agreed that he would be part of the spell and that he would be reduced in size just like Bidu. That way Bidu could keep the clock with her at all times.

"OK, Piru. Cast the spell."

Piru didn't want to risk Bidu's life. She just wanted to go home. But she knew Bidu. She knew Bidu's determination and how much she would want to help. So, she took one of her fairy dust beads and began to cast the spell on Bidu and Gregor. Before she began the spell, Bidu had one more instruction for the girls.

"You need to write a farewell note to Cleopatra. Just tell her thank you and say goodbye. Do not tell her anything about the clock or how we are going back, only that it is time for us to go and we wish her the best.

Once I find Caesarion, we will write that in the note as well."

Piru and Lucinda agreed to this. Piru gave Bidu a hug and then began the spell. "Sweet spirits, please surround Bidu and Gregor in this fairy dust. Make them smaller than a fly so that they will not be noticed. Protect and watch over them and bring them back safely to us. So be it and Amen."

Bidu and Lucinda said "Amen" too as the angels sang. Then, all of a sudden, Bidu was the size of an ant. They could barely see her, she was so small. She began to flap her wings and she headed for the door. Her sore shoulder still hurt, but she tried to ignore it. Then she was gone.

Bidu made her way out of the attendant's area, back to the dining room, and then down the big winding stairs to the dungeon without anyone noticing her because she was so small. Once down in the dungeon, she thought she heard Caesarion crying. She followed the sounds until she found him. He was locked in a different cell than the one the girls had been in. He was way in the back of the dungeon where they stored all of the chains. The guards were trying to wrap a cloth over his mouth so that he couldn't make noise anymore. They were being so mean to him.

"Shut up, you little brat."

Bidu could see that he was really scared.

"I want my mommy," he cried. The guards just laughed.

Bidu wished she could release him somehow, but she was way too small.

"Let's just leave him here until morning. He'll cry himself to sleep. Then we can ask Cleopatra for money to return her son. Once we get the money we will escape and be free."

"Cleopatra will kill us if she finds us. I say let's move him now and get out of this palace. Then we can ask for the ransom."

"You forget. I'm the boss here. I say let's wait until morning and that's what we are going to do."

The other guards just looked at each other. They believed they were right to get out of there as soon as possible, but the other guard was their superior, and they were trained to follow orders even if they didn't agree.

Bidu now knew that they would be there for the night. She flew over to Caesarion and whispered in his ear. "Don't worry, Caesarion, you are safe. Don't talk. Your mother will rescue you soon. Just be quiet and rest." She could tell that he had heard her by his big round eyes. He remained quiet.

She decided that this was the time for her to go back to the other girls. She wished she could somehow tie the guards up, but being the size of an ant meant the best she could do was to be a messenger. She flew as fast as her shoulder would allow, back up the winding stairs, through the dining room, and back into their bedroom. When she got there, no one noticed because she was so small. She had to think about how to get their attention.

She saw Piru writing the note, so she decided to land on the white paper. She didn't want them to think she was just some bug, so she took out the purple velvet bag that held Gregor. Lucinda noticed it first.

"Look, what is that purple speck? Could that be Bidu and the clock?"

"Oh yes!" cried Piru. "She's back. Let me make her big again. Piru took out more fairy dust and reversed the spell. In no time at all, both Bidu and Gregor were back to normal.

"Did you find Caesarion?" asked Piru. "Is he OK? Are you OK?"

"He's fine, just scared. I'm fine too. The guards will keep him in the cell until morning and then they will ask Cleopatra for ransom. We need to warn her."

"We wrote the note, Bidu. Is it OK?" asked Piru.

Bidu read the note that the girls had written:

Dear Cleopatra,

Thank you for your hospitality. We have enjoyed our visit, but now it's time for us to go. We wish you all the best.

Bidu picked up the pen and added the directions to where Caesarion was being held.

Caesarion is being held for ransom in the back of the dungeon where the chains are. The bad guards have kidnapped him. They plan to leave in the morning.

Now Bidu had to think about the best way to get this message to Cleopatra. She didn't really want to leave it in the room because Cleopatra might not come in until morning. So she decided to give the note to the special attendant. First, she told the girls of her plan.

"I will ring for the attendant and give her this note to take to Cleopatra immediately. Then Caesarion can be rescued. While she is delivering the note, we will call Gregor to take us home. Come girls, stand close to me just like we did in Mr. Mayer's clock shop." Once the girls were all close, Bidu rang the bell that called the attendant. She folded the note so that the attendant wouldn't be able to read it first. The attendant came right away.

"Please take this note to Cleopatra immediately. It's about Caesarion."

"Yes, Bidu, right away," replied the attendant. She took the note and moved quickly.

The girls joined hands. They could hear commotion coming from Cleopatra's room and footsteps coming quickly towards them.

Bidu squeezed the hands of her friends. The girls heard the door opening just as she yelled,

"Gregor... Gregor... GREGORRRRRRRRRR..."

10

Girlfriends

A cloud of white smoke surrounded the girls like a warm blanket. They couldn't see at first because there was so much smoke, so they weren't sure where they were landing, but as the smoke cleared, they were so happy to see that they were right back in Mr. Mayer's shop. It was dark there and the shop was obviously closed. They looked out the window and it looked like the sun was just beginning to rise behind the mountains. They figured it must be early morning.

"Oh my goodness, what an adventure!" exclaimed Bidu.

"I wasn't sure we were going to make it out in time," said Piru. "They came so close to stopping us."

Lucinda chimed in. "I know. I do feel a little bad that we didn't say goodbye to the children."

"Yes," said Bidu. "I know what you mean, but it was time for us to go, and we did leave a note. I'm glad we got to see the days of Cleopatra, but I'm happy we live here."

Both Piru and Lucinda nodded in agreement. Just then they heard a key in the door. It was Mr. Mayer coming to work.

"Girls, you're back! How was your adventure?"

"AWESOME!" the girls all said in unison.

Piru asked, "How long were we gone?"

"Well," said Mr. Mayer, for us here it only seemed like you left yesterday, but I bet it felt a lot longer for you! How did it go with Gregor?"

"Oh, Gregor is so amazing," Bidu said. "We couldn't have done this without him."

"So, tell me all about your adventure," said Mr. Mayer excitedly.

The girls took turns telling him everything that had happened, from being captured, to the dungeon, to the big feast, to their escape back home. Even they couldn't believe how crazy some of it sounded.

"It's probably best if you don't tell everyone what has happened because most people won't be able to believe it," Mr. Mayer advised.

"I bet my daddy will," said Bidu. She raised her eyebrows and made a silly face at the other girls and they all started to giggle. That made Mr. Mayer chuckle too.

"Well girls, are you ready to head home now?" he asked.

The girls looked at each other. They wanted to go home and see their families, but they now shared a wonderful bond because of their adventure. They were sad it was over, even though they were so glad to be back home.

"I think we will go to my house first," said Bidu, "and then I'll take Piru and Lucinda back home."

"How will we see each other after we're all back home with our families?" Lucinda asked as her eyes filled with tears.

"Don't worry, Lucinda," Piru said as she took Lucinda's hand. "You and I live close together, but we will have to get Bidu to come to visit more often."

Now Bidu was feeling sad. It was a long walk to Fairyland and soon school would be starting.

"Let's go to my house," Bidu said. "I bet my daddy will know how this will all work out." Right then, she remembered that she still had the clock with her, safe in the purple velvet bag. She started to take off the bag to give it back to Mr. Mayer, but she felt so sad. She had grown to depend on Gregor and having him close made her feel so safe.

Mr. Mayer noticed that Bidu was taking off the bag. He knew what Bidu and the girls were feeling.

"Bidu," he said. "How about you keep the enchanted clock for your journey to take the girls home? Would that make you feel more safe and secure?"

"Oh yes!" cried Bidu.

"Yes, yes, yes!" cried Piru and Lucinda.

Mr. Mayer smiled at the girls and then looked right at Bidu.

"I think you should keep the clock for now. Once your friends are back home, and you're back home safe and sound, there will be plenty of time for you to bring Gregor back. I know you will take good care of him, and I know he will take good care of you too."

"Thank you, Mr. Mayer," said Bidu. "Yes, we will take very special care of Gregor." Piru and Lucinda nodded in agreement.

"Now get going," said Mr. Mayer. "Your parents will be so happy to have you home. Bidu, I'll see you when you get back. Piru and Lucinda, you have a good trip home. You're welcome here anytime. It's been a pleasure meeting you!"

All of the girls gave Mr. Mayer a big hug. As they got to the door, they turned to wave goodbye. Bidu thought she saw a knowing kind of smile on Mr. Mayer's face… like he knew something they didn't know… yet.

****

"Mama, Daddy, we're back!" yelled Bidu as the girls ran up the walkway. Oh, the house looked so good and it felt so great to be home.

Marie ran to the door when she heard Bidu's voice.

"Jim, come quick, the girls are back!" Marie yelled.

"I'm on my way," Jim called. He had been trimming the lemon trees. He wiped his hands and ran into the house. When he saw Bidu, he grabbed her and held her for a long time.

"Oh sweetheart, I'm so happy you're back. Hi, Piru and Lucinda," he said as he opened his arms to give them hugs too.

Both of the girls were happy to be there. Jim made them feel so welcome. They all hugged as Jim invited them to sit down.

"Tell your mother and I everything about your adventure," he said.

"Can I get you girls some fresh lemonade?" asked Marie.

"Oh yes," they all answered at once. They were thirsty, and hungry.

"Did you save any chicken and noodles?" asked Bidu as she laughed.

Marie laughed too. "Well, as it turns out, I never made it because your father came home and said you girls had other plans. But, since it's still morning, Bidu, I bet I could just whip some up in time for dinner tonight."

"Oh, that would be great!" said Bidu. "We're starving."

Jim laughed too and said, "Dinner won't be for a while. So if you girls are hungry, how about I cook up some eggs and bacon to hold you over?"

"What's bacon?" asked Piru.

"Hmmm," said Jim. "I'm not sure exactly how to describe it. Let me go into the kitchen and fix us all a nice big breakfast. You can tell us all about your adventure while we're eating. Why don't you girls go wash up and just relax for a little while out on the porch with your homemade lemonade. It's a beautiful day to be outside."

"Oh Daddy, could we take the lemonade up into the tree house?" asked Bidu.

"Of course, sweetheart."

Marie came in with three tall glasses of lemonade made from the lemons that just came from their lemon trees. She handed a glass to each of the girls and they took them to the tree house.

As they climbed up, they couldn't help thinking of how they came up to the tree house when they first got there. It seemed like so long ago now. They sipped their drinks as they sat out on the deck of the tree house. They talked all about their adventure. They couldn't believe all that had happened since they met.

They were bonded forever.

As they talked and laughed and just enjoyed being together, Bidu got very quiet all of a sudden.

"What's wrong, Bidu?" asked Piru. Piru could always tell when Bidu wasn't herself.

Bidu looked at Piru and Lucinda for a long while before she spoke with tears in her eyes.

"I just realized that soon you girls will be going back to your kingdom. You will still be close to each other, but I will have to come back home. I won't be able to see you like now."

Tears began to roll down Bidu's cheeks. Then Piru, who felt what others felt, started to cry, and Lucinda felt it too. Soon they were all crying. Then for some reason, as they looked at each other, they all started laughing at the same time.

Bidu spoke first. "Oh girls, we have to find a way to see each other. We have been through so much together. It just can't be over."

"No," said Piru. "It can't ever be over."

Lucinda stopped crying. Somehow, she knew it was going to work out, but she didn't know how just yet.

"Girls, breakfast is ready!" called Jim.

The girls dried their eyes and headed down the ladder. They really were hungry. They would talk about this with Bidu's parents. Maybe they would have some ideas.

As they got closer to the house, the wonderful smell of bacon filled the air. Piru and Lucinda didn't recognize that aroma, but they knew for sure that it smelled amazing.

"Come on in, girls. Wash your hands. You're in for a real treat. No one makes better breakfast than Jim," said Marie.

The girls washed and sat down to a delicious breakfast of scrambled eggs, bacon, hash browns and homemade biscuits.

They hadn't realized just how hungry they were until they started gobbling their food. Jim and Marie seemed to be very amused by how fast and furious the girls were eating, but they were happy that the girls loved it so much. No one was talking, as they were so busy enjoying every mouthful.

Once they were all filled up, Jim asked them lots of questions about their adventure. The girls talked and talked. He could tell that Marie wasn't sure what to believe, but Jim reassured her that even though their stories might sound too fantastic to be real, they certainly were real. She began to accept it all and then she listened to every word. Once they had told everything there was to tell about Cleopatra, Bidu told of how they got back and how Mr. Mayer let her keep the clock while she took her friends home. Then Bidu once again, felt sad.

"Daddy, I know I have to take my friends back to their lands, but however will I see them again?"

Her daddy could see her concern. He thought about it for a minute before he spoke.

"Bidu, perhaps we can talk to Mr. Mayer about how the clock might help you see your friends. I'm not sure how that would happen, but why don't we take a walk over there and talk to him?"

Bidu smiled. She liked that idea. Her daddy always had good ideas when she was sad, but she thought that maybe she should just talk with Gregor to see what the possibilities might be. After all, the clock was Gregor's home and he should know what he could do.

"Daddy, may I please be excused?" she asked.

"Yes, of course. Why don't you girls go outside and play while your mother and I clean up. Then we'll all take a walk into town."

"Great!" said Bidu as the girls followed her outside. Bidu told the girls she needed a moment to talk with Gregor. Of course, the girls wanted to go up into the tree house again, so off they went, while Bidu gathered her thoughts to share with Gregor. Once the girls had safely climbed up the ladder, Bidu called to Gregor. She still wasn't used to talking only in her mind, so she called his name out loud. He didn't answer. Then she realized that he only answered in her mind. So, she thought, "Gregor, can you please talk to me?"

"Hello, Bidu. How may I serve you?"

"I'm so upset because I know I have to take my friends home, but then how will I be able to see them again? It takes hours to walk to their land. I have school and other chores. I just don't know what I will do if I can't see them. They live so far away."

"Bidu," Gregor began. "Breathe. No need to get upset. You are my master, and I am here to serve you. As long as I am with you, I can take you anywhere, anytime. No need to walk all that way. If you program me to take you to Fairyland, I can get you there in an instant. The good part for today is that Piru's parents think you have only been gone for a few days, and Lucinda's parents have been under the spell of a wonderful sleep so they won't remember that you have been gone at all!"

"Oh, Gregor!" exclaimed Bidu. "That sounds awesome!"

Bidu suddenly went quiet.

"What is it, Bidu?" Gregor asked. He could feel her sadness.

"Please don't get me wrong, I'm so happy you could do that for me so I can take them home. But then I have to give you back to Mr. Mayer. So how will I see my friends after that?"

"Let's not worry about that just yet," Gregor said. "Let me think about it. You will talk with Mr. Mayer today. He already said you could take me with you for this trip. You might not want to ask for more just yet. Do you understand?"

"I think so," said Bidu. "My daddy tells me how I get ahead of myself sometimes and that patience is something I need to work on."

"Well, I'd say this is an opportunity for you to work on both of those things! Just don't worry. Things have a way of working out just the way they are supposed to."

"OK, Gregor. I know you're right. I feel better now. I'm excited to take you with us for the walk home."

"You mean the ride home, don't you?" And Gregor laughed. This was the first time Bidu ever heard him laugh… it was the cutest laugh she ever heard. It was contagious, so she started laughing too. She loved Gregor.

"Bidu," Gregor said. "I want you to know that whatever happens, I have truly enjoyed being with you. You and your friends have beautiful hearts and you do good things. This will always come back to you. So promise me you will never change. I hope I can always know you and that when I'm no longer with you, you will still come to visit me."

"Oh yes, Gregor. I will always come to visit you. I feel so safe when I have you with me."

"I will protect you always," replied Gregor.

Bidu stroked the purple velvet bag. It was so soft, and she hoped that Gregor could feel her. He could. He could feel everything.

Bidu ran back to tell her daddy that Mr. Mayer had already told her she could take the clock with her to take her friends home.

"You know, Daddy, I am so grateful that Mr. Mayer said I could have Gregor for the trip. I don't want to ask him for more right away. I think I'm getting ahead of myself, like you say, and I just want to appreciate what Mr. Mayer is giving me."

"That's my girl, Bidu. I agree with you. Being grateful for what you have is a gift. So, no need to go into town then. Why not have a relaxing day with your friends; then you will finally get to have your mother's chicken and noodles and a good night's sleep. You can leave first thing in the morning."

"Good idea, Daddy." Bidu felt like this was all good now.

She ran out to the tree house to be with the girls. They laughed and played all day. Bidu had a bike, a scooter, and a skateboard. She showed the girls all of them. They had never seen any of them before. Piru still didn't have great balance on her human legs, but Bidu had an idea. She asked her daddy if her training wheels were still in the garage for the bike. Luckily, they were so Jim put them back on. Lucinda wanted the scooter because it had handles to hold on to, so that left the skateboard for Bidu. The girls had so much fun riding up and down the street.

Then Piru had her own idea.

"Girls, we still have many beads of fairy dust. I would like to ride my bike in the sky. What about you, Lucinda? Wouldn't you like to ride that scooter up high?"

"Oh yes," laughed Lucinda. "That would be so fun!"

"And Bidu… have you ever skateboarded twenty feet off the ground?"

"Never, but I would love to! It's so much fun having a fairy for a friend! Let's do it!"

The girls all laughed and laughed as Piru pulled off one of the beads. Then she stopped.

"What's wrong, Piru?" asked Bidu.

"I almost forgot that I can only use the fairy dust for good and for others. I can give you a new experience, but I won't be able to give it to myself."

"No problem, Piru," said Bidu. "I am still an honorary fairy, so I can make it happen for you too, can't I?"

"Yes, you can!" exclaimed Piru.

They were so happy.

They cast the spells on each other and soon they were sailing in the sky. They stayed in the back yard so that the neighbors wouldn't see so much. They were squealing and laughing as they all rode around each other and over the tree tops. Soon Bidu's parents heard the commotion. They came outside to see what was happening.

At first, they looked all around the yard and didn't see anybody. The girls laughed harder because they thought this was so funny. Then Bidu's mother looked up.

"Oh my, Jim. The girls are flying!" She put her hands on her face. She was so surprised.

"Looks like fun to me!" Jim said as he burst out laughing.

"Follow me," said Bidu. She swooped down towards the ground on her skateboard. Piru and Lucinda followed. They whooshed past her parents as they howled with laughter. Then they all did somersaults in the sky.

"Oh, you girls," said Marie. "You have fun, but try not to bump all the fruit off the trees." She was happy that the girls were having so much fun. She still couldn't believe all that had happened since Bidu met Piru, but she was happy that Bidu had sweet friends. Sometimes Bidu was lonely as an only child, so it made Marie's heart swell to see her daughter so happy.

The girls played until Bidu's daddy came out to call them in for dinner. All that playing had made them hungry again. As they got close to the house, another new wonderful aroma filled their noses.

"Wow!" shrieked Piru. "What's that amazing smell?"

"Finally, you're going to taste my mother's famous chicken and noodles," said Bidu. "It's her most special dinner and now I get to share it with you."

They went inside to wash up. They were ready to eat for sure. Everything they did together was so much fun.

After that amazing breakfast, the girls were anxious to taste this feast. Piru was thinking she would miss Bidu most, but she would miss eating human food almost as much!

Lucinda could barely wait to taste, so she picked up her fork first and took a huge bite. "MMMMMMMMMM, this is unbelievable."

Piru took a bite and she could only say "MMMMMMM".

There wasn't much talking but there were lots of MMMMMMMs, and OOOOOHs, and AAAAAAHs. Of course, Marie was beaming. She loved to cook and when people liked her cooking, she was so happy. She looked up at Jim as he winked at her.

"Another masterpiece meal, honey," he said as he filled his mouth with more noodles.

The girls ate so much and were so full that they could barely move.

"Why don't you girls... you too, Marie, go into the living room and relax while I do the clean up?" Jim smiled a big smile. Bidu loved it when her daddy smiled. It always made her feel good.

They all sat around the fire and talked about the amazing day they just had and their plans for the next day.

"What time will you be leaving tomorrow?" Marie asked.

"We'll go after breakfast if that's OK, Mama."

"Of course that's OK, dear. But feel free to stay as long as you like. I will miss having a house full of girls. And when do you think you'll be back home, Bidu?"

"I should be back by dinner."

Jim heard that and came in from the kitchen.

"Unless of course, they find another unexpected adventure!"

Bidu felt her heart beat just a little faster… another unexpected adventure… whatever could that be?

11

The Thief

The girls woke to the light of the sun and the sound of the birds chirping "good morning" like a song. The aroma of bacon filled the air. All three of them were excited at their upcoming trip with Gregor, but they were also sad that after today, they would not be together every day anymore. They had grown to love and depend on each other like sisters. One thing that amazed them was that even though they were all very different, from different lands and cultures, inside they were all the same. It was like they felt the same about everything and now that they were all close, they knew each other so well. It was wonderful… just wonderful!

"Oooh, I smell bacon," said Piru with a big smile on her face. "I'm going to miss eating human food when I go home!" she exclaimed. "I wonder if I will feel hungry."

"Probably not," said Bidu. "I bet when you're back home, you will just naturally be a fairy like always. But you can remember these times any time you want to."

She really wasn't sure what she was saying was true, but she hoped it made Piru feel better.

Lucinda started to cry. "I'm going to miss you both so much. I never had friends like you two before."

Of course, that made Piru sad too, and then she and Bidu both had tears in their eyes. Bidu went to hug them both when they were interrupted.

"Breakfast is ready, girls," yelled Jim. "Come and get it!"

The girls ran to the table. They all recognized the bacon on their plates, but only Bidu knew what those round things with the little holes were.

"What are those?" asked Lucinda.

"Waffles," answered Bidu laughing. "Have you never heard of waffles?"

Piru was laughing. She thought that was the funniest word ever.

"Waffles, waffles, WAFFLES…"

Piru couldn't stop saying that word. Every time she said it, she burst out laughing. Then Lucinda and Bidu started saying it and laughing too. Jim and Marie were delighted with the joy of the girls, so they joined in too. Soon everyone was saying "waffles," then they were singing "waffles," and then they were all dancing around singing their newly created waffle song.

"I love waffles
waffles love me
time to eat them and fill my tummeeeeee!"

What amazing times they had together.

"Let's eat before it gets cold. No one likes a cold waffle," said Jim, still laughing.

Once again, Piru and Lucinda were blown away by the amazing human food.

"Yummy," said Piru.

"Oh, so good," added Lucinda.

"Well," said Jim. "I'm so happy you enjoy my cooking. You are both welcome here anytime."

"Oh, I hope we can come back again," said Piru.

"I hope so too," said Jim. "Marie and I have really loved having you here."

Marie nodded and smiled. Even she had a little tear in her eye at the thought that the girls would be leaving soon.

They all finished their breakfast with gusto as they made their plans for the day.

"Where should we have Gregor take us first?" asked Bidu.

"Why don't we go to Fairyland first, then we can walk to Lucinda's," suggested Piru.

"OK," said Bidu. "That sounds good."

"Do you girls need to do anything before you go?" Jim asked.

"Not really, Daddy. We just need to get dressed, then tell Gregor where to take us and he does the rest."

"Should we get going?" asked Lucinda.

"I guess it's time," said Bidu.

The girls all said their goodbyes to Jim and Marie. They thanked them many times for their amazing hospitality. Of course, Piru kept thanking them for the food!

"I loved the waffle waffles… and I will never forget the mishmarshalls," said Piru as all the girls mimicked her and laughed. Of course, there were lots of hugs and a few tears. Then they went to change to get ready for their trip.

They decided they would leave from Bidu's room. That way when she came back, she would be in her home. They programmed Gregor to take them to Fairyland as their destination. They put in the date as two days earlier.

"Wait, Bidu," said Piru. "Can you have Gregor drop us just outside of the town?"

"Why is that?" Bidu asked.

"Well, we will need to change into fairies again. I'm afraid we might scare the other fairies if three big human girls just pop up in the middle of the town."

"Will I be a fairy too?" asked Lucinda.

"Yes, Lucinda. I will make you a fairy too, but just for a short time."

"Oh, goody!" shouted Lucinda. "I get to be a fairy!"

"Good idea," said Bidu.

"Is there a name for the area just outside of Fairyland?"

"Yes," said Piru. "It's called Hinterland. No one goes there as it pretty barren."

"Got it!" said Bidu. She reprogrammed Gregor to take them to Hinterland.

They said one more goodbye to Jim and Marie. Finally, Bidu was ready to push the button. She felt very comfortable programming the clock now. At first it seemed almost overwhelming, but now it seemed so easy. She pushed the go button and soon they were surrounded in the white smoke that was now so familiar to them. They felt their feet leave the floor and then, in an instant, they were in the middle of what looked like a desert.

"Wow, there is nothing here at all," said Bidu as she looked all around.

"Do you know how to get to Fairyland from here?" Lucinda asked.

"Oh no," said Piru. "I don't. I've never been here before. The fairies don't ever come here."

They looked in every direction, but they only saw more desert wherever they looked.

Lucinda started to cry. "Oh no, now what will we do?"

"Don't worry Lucinda," Bidu said softly. "I'll just ask Gregor."

"Oh yes, what a great idea," said Piru.

Lucinda was nodding her head.

Bidu remembered to use her mind. That, too, was getting easier the more she did it. She held her hand up so the girls knew not to talk for a moment.

"Gregor?" Bidu called.

"Hello Bidu. How may I serve you?"

"We're lost. Can you help us get to Fairyland?"

"Of course," he said with a chuckle. "It's about a 40 minute walk due west from here."

"Which way is due west?" asked Bidu.

"Hmmm, you will actually have to take a few steps so I can tell you if you're going due west or not."

Bidu relayed the information to the girls.

"Gregor says we have to walk for about 40 minutes. Let's all start walking and then he will be able to tell us if we are going in the right direction."

The girls stood side by side and all started walking in the same direction. The alarm sounded on the clock.

"Wait, wait!" shouted Bidu. "Gregor is sending an alarm. This must not be the right way."

"What is it, Gregor?" asked Bidu.

"You need to turn around. Start walking in the opposite direction. Keep walking and I will send you an alarm if you get off course. It's hard sometimes to keep walking in a straight line when there is nothing to see."

Bidu told the girls. They did an about face and started walking again. This time there was no alarm, so they kept going. Bidu looked at the clock and it said it was 10:35 am. Gregor had said it was about 40 minutes, so she told the girls they should be there before noon for sure.

At about 10:50, the alarm went off. Bidu stopped and told the girls to stop too.

"What is it, Gregor?" she asked.

"You are getting a little off course. Pretend you are walking toward the 12 on a clock. You need to turn slightly to the right and walk more towards two o'clock. Do you understand?"

"Yes, I understand. We still can't see anything but desert."

"Don't worry," said Gregor. "In about 15 minutes more, you will start to see the tops of the trees in Fairyland. Then you can just keep walking towards them."

"OK," said Bidu. "Gregor?"

"Yes, Bidu."

"I'm so glad you're here."

"My pleasure to serve you."

The girls turned right slightly and kept walking as Gregor instructed. Just as he said, after about 15 minutes, they began to see something.

Piru saw it first. "Oh look!" she shouted with joy. "I see something… it looks like our forest!"

Lucinda was so happy; she started clapping her hands.

"Piru, do you know how to find your house once we get to the forest?" Bidu asked.

"I think so. I didn't spend lots of time in the forest. My parents always like me to stay in the village."

Bidu had her concerns, but she felt safe as long as she had Gregor.

She had another question for Piru. "When should we change into fairies?"

"I can change us, no problem," said Piru, "but let's wait until we reach the forest."

"OK, Piru. If you feel that's best," said Bidu.

The girls kept on walking as the trees kept getting closer. The forest was so big and there were so many beautiful trees. It was like the desert, Hinterland, just stopped and the forest began. It was hot in the desert, but as soon as they stepped into the forest, it cooled off. There was nothing to see in the desert, but as soon as they were in Fairyland, it was green and lush. The girls were looking all around enjoying the beauty that surrounded them, when all of a sudden, Gregor sent an alarm. He started talking immediately to Bidu.

"Bidu, you may be in danger. There is a stranger nearby who doesn't belong here."

Bidu was just starting to tell the girls when something jumped out from behind a tree. The girls jumped back and Lucinda screamed. It looked sort of like a man, but instead of arms, he had robot looking things sticking out from his body. His face looked sort of human, but not exactly. He raised his 'arms' into the air, but he didn't move. He was speaking to the girls, but they didn't understand a word. It just sounded like a bunch of gibberish. He kept talking and started waving his 'arms.' The girls didn't understand what was going on.

Gregor spoke to Bidu. "Bidu, stay calm. Tell the girls to stay calm."

Bidu did what Gregor told her to do. Lucinda was crying. Piru was really scared, and Bidu was shaking, but they stood still.

Gregor spoke again. "I recognize his language, Bidu. Do not be scared. He is trying to tell you that he is lost here and that he will not harm you. You need to speak with him. Tell the girls to be quiet."

"How can I speak with him?" Bidu asked. "I don't understand a word he's saying."

"Don't worry," Gregor said. "What you think in English will come out in his language and he will understand you. Once you speak to him, you will then be able to understand what he is saying back to you… just like you did in Egypt."

Bidu didn't know what to say, but she started speaking.

"Who are you and why are you here?"

The robot man's face lit up. He was so happy to talk with someone who understood him.

"I am lost. I am from Xenix. We were here on a mission and I was left behind. I was supposed to meet the mother ship and I was late getting back."

Just then, Bidu thought she recognized the cap he was wearing on his head. Could this be the thief that took Mr. Mayer's clocks?

"Are you the one who took the clocks?"

"Yes," he said. "Are you the girls that I bumped into?"

"Bumped into? More like crashed into."

"I'm sorry. I was scared and alone and lost."

"Why did you take the clocks?" Bidu asked.

"I was trying to find parts so that I could make a transmitter to contact my mother ship. Only one of the clocks looked like it had just what I needed, but I dropped it along the way."

Bidu held tight to Gregor. She was very nervous that if this stranger saw it, he might try to take it. She called to Gregor. Gregor, of course, was right there.

"Hold on to me," he said. "I have a plan. Find out when the mother ship was last here."

Bidu asked the stranger when they were here and what they were doing here.

"We were on a mission to study your soil and plants. You have the same ecosystems that we do, and similar climate. We don't have a lot of foliage so we came to see if we could take cuttings of your plants to take back to Xenix. We meant no harm. We are a peaceful colony."

"Maybe so," said Bidu, "but you can't just come and steal clocks… or anything for that matter. Stealing is not allowed here."

"I'm sorry. It was the only possible way I could get home. I can't stay here. I want to go home."

Bidu started to soften. She had some empathy for him being lost, away from his people.

"Gregor, is he dangerous?"

Gregor answered, "No, Bidu, he is harmless. I think there is a way we might be able to help him get back, but don't say anything just yet."

Piru and Lucinda just stood frozen while Bidu had a conversation with the stranger. They too could understand what was being said, but they had no idea what to do.

Piru decided to ask the stranger a question. "What is your name?"

"My name is Gronk," he said. "What's yours?"

"I'm Piru. This is Lucinda."

"And I'm Bidu."

"Can you help me get home?" asked Gronk.

"I'm not sure just yet. Can you tell me when your mother ship was here?"

"It was four sunsets ago. After I got the clocks, I ran and ran until I hid here. I tried to make a transmitter from these clocks, but I can't get it to work. I don't have the right pieces."

Bidu thought for a minute. "Won't your friends see that you are gone and come back for you?" she asked.

"They won't know where to come because I'm no longer at the launch site. I don't know what to do."

Gregor called to Bidu. "Bidu, I think we can make this work for him. He said he has been here for four sunsets. That would be four days. Ask him how long the mother ship was here and where it was stationed."

"Gronk, how long was the mother ship here before it left?" Bidu asked.

"We were here on our study mission for eight sunsets."

"And where exactly were you stationed?"

"We were in a large park with a big hole with water, but we were invisible so no earthlings could see us. We were parked right next to the big water hole."

Bidu thought for a moment. "That sounds like the same park where we bumped into him. It has a big lake."

"OK, Bidu, I know what we need to do," Gregor said. "We need to go back in time six days. You will need to program me to that park on the date six days ago. Do you know the name of that park?"

"Oh yes," said Bidu. "I play there all the time. But why six days, Gregor? He said he's only been lost for four days."

"Yes, but just to be sure, let's go back six days to when the mother ship was definitely parked there. Tell the girls they won't be going home just yet. Then, program me and let's help him get back to his mother ship. Speak to the girls in English and tell them what we are doing. I don't want Gronk to know what we are planning until it happens. Have them keep Gronk busy talking while you take me out to program me. Don't let him see me. Do you understand why?"

"Yes," said Bidu. "He will want your parts to make a transmitter."

"Right," Gregor answered. "Explain this to the girls. It's very important that they keep him occupied while you are programming me."

Bidu told the girls their trip home was going to be delayed. "Why?" asked Piru. "What's wrong?"

"Don't worry girls. We just have a small delay in our plans. Gregor says we can take Gronk back to his mother ship so he can go home."

Piru and Lucinda were mostly worried about their parents, but they knew this had to be done. Bidu instructed them in English to engage Gronk in conversation while she turned away to program Gregor. Piru told Gronk she had a surprise for him and that he needed to turn around and close his eyes.

Gronk wasn't sure about this, but he did like surprises, so he turned around. That gave Bidu the time she needed to program Gregor. The white smoke surrounded them all and they were lifted and transported back in time six days to the park.

"You can open your eyes now, Gronk," said Piru.

Gronk opened his eyes. He blinked a bunch of times. He couldn't believe what he was seeing.

"Oh my, there is my mother ship!" he exclaimed.

"I can't see anything," Bidu said.

"I told you," said Gronk, "it's invisible to anyone from Earth."

"Gregor, do we need to tell him anything about what day it is or how he got back here?"

"No, Bidu. Tell him he can go home now. It's like we turned the clock back and they won't even know he was lost. Maybe you can sprinkle a little fairy dust to erase his memory too?"

"Gronk," said Bidu, "we would like to send you off with a little prayer before you go."

"Wouldn't you like to come to see the mother ship? My colony will be happy you brought me back."

Gregor broke in. "Not a good idea, Bidu. There would have to be too much explaining and I would be at great risk. Please send him on his way."

Bidu understood. She turned to Piru.

"Piru, can you please do a special blessing for Gronk?"

Of course, Piru knew exactly what Bidu was thinking and Bidu told her in English to erase Gronk's memory. She told Gronk to close his eyes and not to open them until she told him to. Gronk agreed. He closed his eyes tightly as Piru gave a beautiful blessing that Gronk could understand. She ended it in English with the memory erasing and sprinkling of fairy dust.

Gregor spoke, "Bidu, now quickly run with the girls and hide behind the boathouse. He won't know you now that his memory has been erased."

The girls did exactly as Gregor instructed. They hid behind the boathouse that was nearby. Then Piru yelled, "OK, Gronk. Open your eyes."

Gronk opened his eyes, but he had no idea as to what had just happened. He only knew the mother ship and began running towards it. Now he would be safe.

"I wish we could have seen the mother ship," said Bidu, "but I know we had to keep Gregor safe and that's the most important thing."

The girls agreed. They would never want to put Gregor at risk.

"Wow!" exclaimed Piru. "Even though I was so scared at first, that was amazing to meet someone from another planet."

Lucinda agreed. Bidu started to giggle.

"What's so funny, Bidu?" Piru asked.

"I guess you could call what just happened an 'unexpected adventure' just like my daddy said."

Now Piru and Lucinda started giggling too. "I still wish we could have seen the mother ship," Piru said.

"Me too," said Lucinda.

"Me three!" said Bidu, which brought on lots more giggles and laughter.

Gregor reminded Bidu that they still had to get Piru and Lucinda back home. "Do not put in Hinterland this time, Bidu. Instead, I have the coordinates of the forest. Since we came back six days to bring Gronk home, we need to go forward six days to where we were."

"Oh, this is so confusing," Bidu said.

"It's not that confusing," said Gregor. "Just put in what I tell you and it'll be easy."

Bidu knew he was right so she just followed his instructions and once again the girls were bathed in the wonderful white smoke they had all come to love. In an instant, they were back in the beautiful forest. They were feeling relieved and more relaxed, but it didn't last very long. The smoke was just clearing. They all saw what was in front of them as Lucinda let out the loudest scream ever heard...

12

Alicorn Magic

The girls stood frozen as they watched three huge magnificent white-winged horses flying towards them. Bidu saw the single horns on their foreheads and knew instantly what she was seeing, even though she couldn't believe it.

"Lucinda, stop screaming. There is nothing to be afraid of. You'll scare the Alicorns."

Lucinda was shaking with fear. She had never seen anything like this before. And Piru too, was just standing in awe. They remained quiet as the Alicorns circled around above them. It was breathtaking to see these amazing creatures. Bidu knew all about Alicorns. They were another one of her favorite animals, but she never knew they truly existed other than in the stories she had read about them.

"Girls, just relax and be quiet. These are Alicorns. I actually thought they were just mythical magical creatures found only in books. This is an amazing moment. We don't want to scare them."

"Look how big they are," Lucinda blurted out. "They could stomp us with one hoof."

Piru didn't know what to say, but she felt the same feeling as when the angels came to her whenever she cast a spell. She didn't feel afraid at all. Bidu was so thrilled to be seeing this sight that she couldn't take her eyes off the Alicorns. They looked like big beautiful white horses with huge wings and a single horn like a unicorn, but they were about three times bigger than any horse she had ever seen. They all watched as the Alicorns slowly and softly landed about twenty feet in front of them. There was a lead Alicorn and the other two right behind it. They had not seen a sight like this ever before in their lives… not even in their dreams.

The lead Alicorn came forward slowly so as not to scare the girls. Bidu called to Gregor in her mind.

"Gregor?"

"Yes, Bidu. How may I serve you?"

"Can you speak Alicorn?"

Gregor chuckled. "You can just speak English, Bidu. These are magical creatures. They can speak any language. Just start talking to them so they hear that you speak English and they will talk to you in your language. They are very powerful creatures, but very gentle. Speak in a low and calm voice."

Bidu told the girls to remain calm and not to move around too much or run away. She tried to reassure them that they were safe. Lucinda and Piru nodded in understanding as Bidu turned her complete attention to the Alicorns.

"Hello," she said softly.

"Hello," said the lead Alicorn. "My name is Aurora. And this is Astra and Eldora. There is no need to be afraid. We will not harm you."

Bidu smiled. "We know that you are gentle creatures. We are too. My name is Bidu and these are my friends Piru and Lucinda."

Lucinda was shaking as she said, "Oh my, you are so big."

"Hello, Lucinda. Please don't be scared. And Piru, you too are a magical creature. We love fairies."

"How did you know I'm a fairy?" asked Piru. "I'm in a little girl's body right now."

"We know," replied Aurora. "We have been watching you and how kind and helpful you have been on your adventures. We rarely show ourselves to anyone in this world, but you are very special so we wanted to meet you."

"Where are you from?" asked Bidu. "How did you get here?"

Aurora smiled, then slowly began. "We come from a magical place. It's called Syrius. It's a star that is far, far away from here."

"How did you get here?" asked Bidu.

"Why, we flew, of course. We can fly faster than the speed of light so we can go anywhere pretty quickly. We almost just have to think where we want to go, and then poof, we are there!"

"Oh," said Bidu. "Sort of like we do with Gregor?"

"Exactly," said Aurora. "Just like Gregor."

Bidu thought for a moment. "Do you know Gregor?" she asked.

"Why yes, we do. We send thoughts through our minds. He told us all about you and what amazing beings you are."

Lucinda had completely calmed down now, and Piru was just amazed that she was standing with these awesome creatures. Bidu had lots more questions, but it was like Aurora could read her mind.

"I bet you have lots of questions about so many things and I will be happy to answer all of them. Gregor would have a lot of answers as well."

Bidu didn't know that Gregor could actually communicate with Alicorns... or magical creatures from faraway lands. But then, she did think of Gregor as magical too, so it stood to reason that he could communicate with magical creatures, or anyone for that matter.

Her thoughts were interrupted by Aurora's sweet voice.

"Would you girls like to ride with us for a while?"

"You mean on your backs?" asked Lucinda.

Aurora giggled. "Yes, of course. Just like you're riding a horse."

"Oh," said Lucinda. "I've never been on a horse, not really, except for the time we were captured in Egypt, but that wasn't really a fun ride... but riding on you... now that sounds like fun. One time we used fairy dust to fly at Bidu's house. I love to fly!"

The Alicorns were all giggling at Lucinda going on and on, but then Aurora noticed that Piru seemed a bit concerned about something.

"What is it, Piru?" asked Aurora. "You seem concerned."

"Well," said Piru, "I was just wondering how we would get on your backs. You are so big."

"Close your eyes and see yourself being lifted onto our backs. Bidu, you get on me. Piru, you get on Astra, and Lucinda, you get on Eldora. Just imagine it happening. See it in your mind and it will happen. Try it, but have no doubts. Know that it will happen."

The girls all closed their eyes. Bidu was the first one to land up on Aurora's back. Then Piru landed on Astra. Lucinda was still standing on the ground.

"Oh no! Something has gone wrong," she said.

"Lucinda," said Aurora. "You are having doubts about something. What is it?"

"I was just thinking that you are so big. What if I fall off?"

Aurora smiled. "You mustn't worry. Once you are on Eldora, you cannot fall off, no matter what. You just hold on to her mane and it's the most powerful glue ever. You will be completely safe. You must believe this with absolute certainty. Now try it again."

"OK," said Lucinda as she closed her eyes tightly. She took a deep breath and then focused. She could feel herself floating up to Eldora's back.

"I did it. I did it!" she exclaimed.

They all giggled and settled in as they held on to the Alicorns' manes. They could feel the manes wrap around their hands, up their arms, and around their backs. They felt secure.

"Are you ready?" asked Aurora.

"Oh yes!" said Bidu. Piru and Lucinda were nodding in agreement.

"Let's go!" they all said at the same time.

The Alicorns began slowly lifting off the ground. As they lifted higher, their manes wrapped completely around each girl to hold them securely and safely in place.

Bidu thought she heard music and angels singing. The air was cool and it felt so good blowing through her hair. She closed her eyes and just let herself go, flying with Aurora. It was a smooth, joyful ride. She looked around for Piru and Lucinda on their Alicorns. They both looked happy too. They couldn't talk because they were too far away from each other to hear, but all three girls had big smiles. They all felt like they could ride forever. After about an hour, they began slowing down. Bidu looked down but it didn't look anything like Earth to her. They were obviously somewhere else and coming in to land. The ground was so lush and green with flowers, like the most beautiful garden ever. Coming to meet them were hundreds of Alicorns. They made a big circle with an area in the center. They waited as Aurora, Astra, Eldora and the girls came in for a soft landing in the middle of the circle.

"Girls," said Aurora. "Welcome to Syrius. These are all of the Alicorns left in the universe. We used to be on Earth, but sorcerers and magicians hunted us for our wings, our manes and our horns. We almost became extinct. There was no safe place for us."

"Oh no!" exclaimed Bidu. "So how did you come to be on Syrius?"

"There was a famous magician named Merlin. He lived many, many years ago. He respected us and watched out for us. He could see what was happening, but he couldn't stop it. So, he took a big risk to use his magic to transport all that was left of us to Syrius where we could be safe and no one would know where we had gone."

"How did he get you to Syrius?" asked Piru.

"The soldiers found where we lived on Earth. One day they came to hunt us all. They asked Merlin to help them find us, and that is how he knew what was going to happen. He told the soldiers that he would go out first to see where we were hiding, and then come back to get them."

"You mean he was going to help them capture you all?" asked Bidu.

"No, Bidu," Aurora said gently. "Merlin was always our friend. As the soldiers waited for him to report back, he came to warn us and carry out his own plan to save us. He had a good idea and we trusted him to help us. He used all of his powers to make us the size of ants. We all fit into one of the two big pockets of his magician's robe."

Aurora hesitated for a moment. She wasn't sure about telling the girls the next part, but she decided that it would be fine, so she continued. "In the other pocket, he had what he called 'an enchanted clock'."

"Oh my!" exclaimed Bidu. "Do you mean a clock like our enchanted clock?"

Aurora looked lovingly at Bidu as she said, "Bidu, I mean that your clock is exactly the same enchanted clock that Merlin used."

All three girls were silent. They didn't know what to say. Then Lucinda began. "You really mean that our enchanted clock was there with you and Merlin? Gregor was in the clock? He was always in the clock?"

"Yes, Lucinda. Gregor has always been with that clock. He is the clock and he's what makes the clock enchanted. Merlin could not have gotten us to safety without Gregor. He helped Merlin transport us to Syrius which was the only star we could survive on without anyone being able to find us."

"So how did it happen exactly?" asked Bidu.

Aurora continued. "Merlin made us the size of ants and put us all in his pocket. Then he went back to the soldiers and told them he couldn't find us. The soldiers didn't believe him, so they threw him in the dungeon until he would tell them where all the Alicorns had gone. They left Merlin alone in a dark cell. It was there that Merlin programmed Gregor and within minutes, we were all safely here. One day we were on Earth and the next day we were just gone. The soldiers looked for us for a long time, but we were never found because we were no longer there. Now, very few on Earth believe that we are real or that we ever existed. They just tell the story like it's a fairy tale."

Piru started to laugh. "A fairy tale?" she said. "That's funny!" The girls all giggled. So did the Alicorns.

"I'm so sorry that no one believed in you," said Lucinda.

"I have always believed in Alicorns," Bidu said. "And unicorns too."

"And fairies too!" said Piru. The girls giggled even more.

"What happened to Merlin?" asked Bidu.

Aurora answered. "He came with all of us, holding us safely in his pocket. When we got to Syrius, he changed us back into Alicorns. Once he knew we were all safe and accounted for, he had to go back so that he wouldn't be missing from the cell.

"Oh, I know," said Lucinda. "He set the clock back, right?"

"Yes, Lucinda. He set the clock back so they never knew he was missing. After keeping him locked up for many weeks while they searched and searched for us, the soldiers decided that Merlin had told them the truth, so they let him out. Merlin and the soldiers never spoke of this again."

"So how did you find us?" asked Bidu. "Wasn't it dangerous for you to come back to Earth?"

"Gregor knew that what we missed most about Earth was the children. We used to run with them and play with them. One day, Gregor told us about you and your loving hearts. He said you believed in fairies and the unbelievable. He told us how amazing you all are, how you always want to help make situations better. None of us have been back to Earth since Merlin transported us here thousands of years ago, but we missed seeing the children so much. When Gregor described you as being so special, we decided to take a chance. We felt safe with Gregor. We had to bring you here to our land, because it wouldn't be safe for us to stay on Earth very long."

"Oh, that is so sad," said Bidu.

Piru had tears in her eyes. She knew what it was like to be hunted, mistreated, and misunderstood as a fairy. She never really trusted anyone in the human world until she met Bidu.

"We are not sad today," said Aurora. "Today we celebrate you being on Syrius." With that, all of the Alicorns came closer and began to make beautiful music, like songs from angels. The girls were mesmerized by the sounds as their hearts filled with a love they'd never felt before. They had no fear, no concerns, no doubts... only a feeling of calm, peace, and a certainty that all was well.

"I suggest you girls stay up on our backs for a moment," said Aurora. You will be able to see everyone better from up high. I can tell you that all of us are so happy to have you here. Now let's have you meet everyone."

Aurora, Astra, and Eldora slowly walked all around so that the girls could get close enough to some of the Alicorns to say hello and pet their soft coats. Their manes were like silk, soft and flowing, so long and beautiful. Every one of the Alicorns nuzzled each girl. What amazing, loving creatures they were.

"Now that you have met everyone, we want you to know that the one thing we miss the most is watching the children dance to our music. Do you girls like to dance?"

"Oh yes!" said Bidu.

"Yes, yes!" exclaimed Piru and Lucinda.

"OK then," said Aurora. "Hold onto our manes and we will lower you to the ground. You can dance in that little area right over there." She pointed to a large open area with soft grass.

The girls were gently lowered down as the Alicorns began their amazing music. The girls started moving with overflowing joy. They closed their eyes and felt every note that the Alicorns sang.

"If the music makes you want to fly, you have the power to do so while we are singing," said Astra.

"Yes," said Aurora. "Just let yourself be transported. See your movements in your mind and they will happen."

The girls started twirling and moving to the music. Bidu lifted her arms as she imagined flying in time to the music. As soon as she thought it, it happened!

"Piru, Lucinda!" she shouted. "Think about flying and twirling in the air. Come up here with me. It's so awesome!"

Piru was used to flying as a fairy, but it was very different as a human girl. She pretended that her arms were wings as she flapped them to the music. Soon she was lifted into the air.

Lucinda closed her eyes. She had to clear her mind to focus on everything being just fine. It took her a little while, but soon she, too, was dancing in the air with the other girls. Some of the Alicorns got up on their hind legs and danced too. It was the most magical moment the girls had ever had. They wished it would never end. They all sang and danced for hours, every minute more amazing than the next. The time just flew by when all of a sudden, Gregor sent an alarm to Bidu. She was startled because she didn't think there could ever be a situation of danger on Syrius with the Alicorns.

"Yes, Gregor, what's wrong?" she asked.

"No emergency or danger, Bidu. I just want to let you know that we should be heading back so it will still be today when you get home."

Aurora knew it was time. In fact, all of the Alicorns knew it was time.

"Girls, what a wonderful gift we have had being together. We will never forget you and all the joy you have brought to us."

Bidu thought she saw a single tear slowly drop from Aurora's eye.

"Will we ever see you again?" asked Bidu as she held back her own tears.

"I"m sure we will see each other again," said Aurora softly. "I'll bet Gregor will bring you."

"Oh, Aurora," said Bidu. "Mr. Mayer is the master of the clock. He just let me use it. I have to return Gregor when I get back home." Bidu couldn't hold back her tears any longer. They flowed like a river.

Aurora nuzzled Bidu, and then spoke in her soothing voice. "Remember, Bidu, things always work out just the way they are supposed to. Always have certainty and know that all is well. I believe that we will see each other again. You believe it too. We might not know how or when at this moment, but I hold this thought in my heart."

"I will hold it in my heart too, Aurora."

"Me too," said Piru, wiping her own tears away.

"Me three!" said Lucinda, trying to lighten the moment. It worked. Everyone had a good laugh. Then, instead of feeling sad, they were all happy that they had been able to meet and be together for this day. There were more hugs, nuzzling and sweet farewells. Bidu programmed Gregor to take them back to the forest just outside of Fairyland. She looked up at Aurora and all of the Alicorns one last time. Then she pushed the button.

****

Once again, the girls found themselves surrounded by white smoke, but when it cleared, they were alone in the forest.

They just stood still for a moment, trying to absorb all that had just happened. It almost seemed like a dream, but deep down they all knew that they had just danced with Alicorns and that they were real, just like fairies are real. It seemed like all three girls were thinking the same thing.

"Can you believe what we just did? It really happened, didn't it?" asked Lucinda.

"Lucinda, I'm a fairy, don't forget," said Piru. "If you can believe that I'm real, then you can believe what we just saw is real too. Right, Bidu?"

Bidu giggled. "You mean to tell me that fairies are real?" Bidu asked. "I thought all this time I was just imagining you. Or maybe I am just dreaming."

Piru thought for a moment, and then realized Bidu was just teasing her. She started to laugh and she couldn't stop. Then Lucinda started to laugh too. It was contagious, because soon Bidu was laughing too.

Once again, Bidu heard the alarm from Gregor. "I know, I know, Gregor. We're ready. Can you guide us the shortest way to Piru's house?"

"Of course, Bidu. Are you going to change into fairies so you don't scare half the town?"

"Oh, I almost forgot that little detail," said Bidu, still trying to recover from all of that wonderful laughter.

Gregor continued. "If you all change into fairies, I can transport you right to Piru's house. Why walk when you can ride?"

Piru became quiet. Bidu could sense her. "What's wrong, Piru?"

"I just realized that I don't know when I'll see you again. This might be the last time I change us into fairies."

Bidu spoke softly to Piru and Lucinda. "Girls, did you hear Aurora? We need to have certainty and know that all is well. We have to believe that we will see each other again. We have to believe it with all of our hearts."

Piru and Lucinda nodded and then the girls had a good long hug.

Piru began her spell to change them all into fairies. "Sweet spirits, we have so much gratitude and appreciation for all we have experienced. Please allow us all to be fairies one more time, but please let it not be the last time. We will hold all the love and thoughts of reuniting in our hearts and we will continue to spread love and goodness, so this spell is all for good.

Bidu, Lucinda, please spread the fairy dust."

As the girls sprinkled the fairy dust, Piru ended the spell as the songs of the angels filled the air.

"Thank you, sweet spirits. And so it is. Amen."

Together, Bidu and Lucinda said, "Amen."

They hadn't been fairies for so long that they couldn't believe how close they were to the ground now. They felt smaller than ever before. Even Piru noticed it. They all found it interesting that even Gregor was fairy size. Whatever size the girls were, that's the size the clock was. That made it so much easier to program it! Bidu put in Piru's address.

"Gregor, do I put today's date?"

"Yes, Bidu. We will be there in an instant."

Bidu pushed the button and again they were surrounded in white smoke. They never got tired of the wonderful white smoke. They landed on the front lawn of Piru's house. When her parents saw the smoke, they came running out.

As the smoke cleared and the girls appeared, Piru's parents were so happy.

They recognized Piru, of course, and they recognized Bidu as a fairy, but who was this stranger? They had never seen Lucinda as a fairy before. Piru explained that Lucinda had secretly followed them and that they couldn't turn back to bring her back to Fairyland because they didn't want the spell to end.

"We wondered why you never came back here, Lucinda. Now we understand. You're parents must be worried sick."

"No, it's OK," said Lucinda. "Piru put a spell on them so they haven't missed me at all."

"Well, that was definitely not the plan, but good thinking on your part Piru. What kind of spell did you put on them?"

"It was a sleeping spell. They are having sweet dreams now until Lucinda gets home and wakes them with a kiss."

Piru's parents weren't particularly happy but they seemed to understand. After all, they were fairies too, and they knew of spells and all that fairies could make happen. For now, they were just so happy to see their daughter that they didn't really care to hear every little detail.

"We're just glad you're back safe and sound. Why don't you all come in and sit for a while?"

"Mom, Lucinda has to get back home soon, but we will come inside for just a minute."

They all went into the cozy living room. Lucinda was happy to fit inside this time! It felt good to have a little down time after the whirlwind of adventures they had just been on. Piru couldn't wait to tell her parents everything, but not today.

After the girls had rested awhile, Bidu suggested that she take Lucinda home. She really wished she could stay and hear more of Dartu's wonderful stories, but she knew that would have to wait until another visit. Lucinda really did need to get back home and so did she. Of course, that meant that Piru would have to change them back to their real sizes. Piru went over to Bidu and gave her a big fairy hug.

"Oh, Bidu. You are the best friend I have ever had. You saved me when I was hurt. You saved me from the fairy snatchers and the Egyptian soldiers. You have watched out for me and taken care of me and I will never forget you."

Then she went over to Lucinda. "Lucinda, I'm so glad we met and that you were able to come with us on the most amazing adventures. You and I will see each other since we are only a few villages apart. I know we will be friends forever too."

Then Piru turned her attention back to Bidu. "I don't know how or when I will get to see you again, but I know it will happen. I will miss you every day and I will send you messages in my mind."

"Don't worry, Piru. I know we are forever friends and fairy sisters. We will see each other again... I might not know when right now, but I will figure this out somehow. Just know that I love you and I will love you even if I don't see you."

"Me too," said Piru as she wiped a tear away.

"Me three!" shouted Lucinda who always thought that was so funny to say. The girls all had another good laugh and one more long embrace as fairies and a few more tears. Then it was time for Piru to cast the spell that would return them back to their original forms. Of course, she had to make the spell outside or the girls would be wearing Piru's fairy house on their heads!

The girls said their goodbyes to Piru's parents, then one more goodbye to each other.

"Wait, Bidu!" shouted Piru as she removed her necklace with the fairy dust.

"Please take this with you."

There were still lots of beads full of the magic dust. She reminded Bidu that she would always have the little honorary fairy wings on her back. That made Bidu feel so good. It made her feel like she would stay close to Piru even when they were apart.

Just before the girls turned and walked away, Piru called to Lucinda.

"Lucinda, don't forget there is a spell on your parents. When you get home, all you need to do is to go to them and kiss them gently and they will wake up as if you have never been gone."

Lucinda nodded that she understood.

Bidu took Gregor out of the soft purple bag that was always over her shoulder.

Luckily, Lucinda knew the address of the big castle, so they decided to have Gregor take them there and then they would finish walking inside to Lucinda's house. Lucinda smiled as she saw the white smoke. She was going to miss it because it always meant something exciting was happening. In just the blink of an eye, they found themselves right in front of the castle. Bidu could remember every detail of her first visit here and the wonderful feast. She would miss Lucinda too and looked forward to a day when all three of them might be able to go on a new adventure together. They walked holding hands to Lucinda's house.

Lucinda went into her parents' bedroom. She kissed her mother first, then her father. They slowly awoke and were so happy to see their daughter. As they came out into the living room they noticed Bidu.

"And who is this?" they said looking at Bidu.

"Don't you remember?" Lucinda said. "Bidu was at the big feast."

She forgot to mention that when they met, Bidu was a fairy.

"Oh yes," said her parents. You would think we would remember since it was just last night, but there has been so much going on, it must have just slipped our minds. Welcome, Bidu."

Lucinda decided to just forget the fairy part for now!

"Thank you. I won't be able to stay long because my parents are waiting for me too. Maybe I can come back another time to visit."

"Oh, that would be lovely dear. We're so glad that Lucinda has made a new friend. She has been pretty shy as you may have noticed."

"I think she's quickly overcoming that!" laughed Bidu as she gave a knowing look to Lucinda. Lucinda laughed too. Her parents weren't quite sure what they found so funny, but they gave a little chuckle or two as well. They were just happy that their daughter had a friend.

"Well, Lucinda, I really do have to get going," said Bidu.

"Try not to tell your parents every little thing in one night."

"I know. They probably wouldn't believe me anyway. I didn't exactly have an exciting life before I met you and Piru."

She grabbed Bidu and gave her the longest hug. "I love you, Bidu."

"I love you too, Lucinda."

Lucinda walked Bidu to the front entrance of the castle and watched as she walked off into the distance. She felt sad and happy at the same time. Sad that Bidu was leaving but happy that she got to meet her. She would practice knowing that they would see each other again. She had learned so much from Bidu and Piru. For that, she would be eternally grateful.

Once out of sight, Bidu took out the enchanted clock that had changed her life in so many ways. She realized that this could very well be the last time she would program Gregor and be transported.

"Gregor?"

"Yes, Bidu. How may I serve you?"

"I'm really going to miss you."

"I understand, Bidu. I will miss you as well. I hope you will come and visit me sometimes."

"Oh yes, I will. I was going to have you take me home, but I feel like I should take you back to Mr. Mayer now. I bet he's missed you too."

"Yes, I bet he has. He is a good master and I am grateful that he allowed me to be with you for these adventures."

Bidu slowly programmed Gregor. She never wanted this to end, but she knew it was time. She put in the destination of Mr. Mayer's clock shop. They would go back to where they started.

"Bidu, just enter the real date. No need to turn me back anymore now."

"OK, Gregor," she replied.

"Gregor?"

"Yes, Bidu."

"Thank you for everything."

"My pleasure, Bidu. You are an amazing spirit. It has been a true joy to know you."

She tried to focus on all of the wonderful adventures and all of the amazing experiences she'd had instead of how sad she was that it was over. She finished the programming and pushed the button. She wished she could stay in the beautiful white smoke for a long time, but as always, it was just a few seconds. As the smoke cleared, she could tell they were back in Mr. Mayer's shop, but she didn't see Mr. Mayer. He always came out front. She felt her heart beating as if something might not be right. She called out. "Mr. Mayer? We're back."

Nothing happened. Mr. Mayer did not come.

"Gregor, I don't see him."

"Go and look in the back room. He might be doing some repairs."

Bidu rushed back to the repair room and as she looked around, she felt all the blood drain from her face as she saw Mr. Mayer lying on the floor. He was unconscious…

13

The Gift

"Mr. Mayer, Mr. Mayer!" cried Bidu. But there was no answer. He didn't move or speak or open his eyes. Bidu could tell that he was still breathing. She knew how to call 911 in an emergency and she also knew how to perform CPR because her father had made sure she learned how when her grandma lived with them.

"911, what is your emergency?" asked the voice on the phone.

"Mr. Mayer is not moving. He's on the floor, but he's still breathing. Please hurry. He needs help."

"Please stay on the line. We are sending help right away."

The dispatcher on the line talked with Bidu the entire time until the ambulance arrived. She stayed calm and made Bidu feel so much better, although Bidu was a little scared. This reminded her of the time her grandma had a heart attack and her daddy had to call the ambulance. Bidu knew this was serious, but she didn't know how serious. She could hear the sirens in the distance, so she knew that the ambulance would be there very soon. She heard the siren get louder and louder, and then suddenly stop. They were here! Bidu ran to the front door to guide them in.

"He's right in the back… this way."

The attendants brought in a big white stretcher. One of them carried a black bag of medical supplies. They asked all kinds of questions, but Bidu didn't know anything more than what happened from the time she arrived and found Mr. Mayer already on the floor. She had no idea what had happened before that.

They listened to his heart and took his pulse. They put an IV into his arm so they could begin giving him fluids. This, too, reminded Bidu of the time they came to get her grandma. She felt sick to her stomach. Mr. Mayer was such a nice man. She didn't want anything terrible to happen to him.

"Is he going to be OK?" asked Bidu.

One of the attendants answered. "We need to get him to the hospital, but don't worry. We will do everything we can for him. Do you know if he has any family we can call?"

"I'm not sure," said Bidu. "I've never heard him speak of family."

Then Bidu went into her mind to speak with Gregor. "Gregor, does Mr. Mayer have any family?"

"No, Bidu. He is alone. He was married for a long time, but his wife passed away some years ago. They didn't have any children, so there is no one that I know of."

"Oh," said Bidu. "I'm sad for him. We will have to make sure he is taken care of. I'm going to call my parents right now."

"That is a good thing, Bidu, and just like you to want to help."

Bidu called home. Her father answered.

"Oh, Daddy, something terrible has happened."

"What is it, Bidu?"

She explained how she came back to return the clock and found Mr. Mayer on the floor. She told him that the ambulance was getting ready to take him to the hospital right now.

"Can you ride with Mr. Mayer and I will meet you at the hospital?"

Bidu asked the attendants if she could go with Mr. Mayer and they said she could ride up front.

"Yes, Daddy. I can go in the ambulance."

"OK then, try to stay calm. I will meet you at the hospital."

Bidu held tightly onto Gregor. She watched as they took Mr. Mayer out on the stretcher and put him into the back of the ambulance. Then she got up in the front because the attendant was staying in the back with Mr. Mayer.

The sirens were again turned on and they were on their way to the emergency room. If Bidu hadn't been so concerned about Mr. Mayer, she would have thought riding in an ambulance was pretty cool. Since Mayville was a small town, there was only one hospital, so she knew exactly where they were going. They were there quickly. As soon as they pulled in, more attendants came out of the emergency room to help get Mr. Mayer inside safely.

"Bidu, you can just wait in the waiting room until we get him settled," one of the attendants said.

"OK," said Bidu. Oh, how she wished her father would get there. And just like that she saw him rushing in through the big glass sliding doors.

"Oh, Daddy, I'm so glad you're here." She grabbed him and held him for a long time.

"It's going to be OK, Bidu. Try not to worry. You did all the right things to help him."

"Daddy, did you know Mr. Mayer has no family?"

"Yes, Bidu, he had a lovely wife, but she died several years ago. You probably don't remember her because you were a lot younger then. So, yes, he is mostly alone."

Bidu's eyes filled with tears. "We just can't let him be all alone through this. We have to be there for him. He's such a nice man."

"Don't worry, Bidu. We won't let him feel alone. Right now, we don't know what he might need, so let's wait until we know more."

He held his precious daughter close. He was always so proud of her and her sweet heart.

They sat down in the waiting room. They waited for what seemed like a long time. Then a doctor came out.

"Who is here for Mr. Mayer?" he asked.

Bidu jumped up. "We are!" she announced. "Is Mr. Mayer going to be OK?"

The doctor smiled. "Yes. He is in serious condition, but he will be OK. He has had a mild heart attack, but with time he should heal just like new. He will need rest and some rehabilitation, a healthy diet and of course, lots of love and kindness. Are you his family?" the doctor asked.

Jim put his hand on Bidu's shoulder. She knew that meant he wanted to talk right now.

"Mr. Mayer doesn't have any family. We are his friends."

"Well," said the doctor, "he really shouldn't be alone for awhile because he will need some special care. We can make arrangements for him to go to a care facility."

"Oh Daddy, we just can't send him to one of those hospital-like places. Can't we take him home with us and let him stay in Grandma's old room? I'll take care of him and read to him so he won't feel so alone. Please, Daddy!" cried Bidu.

"Bidu, I know your heart. But I do have to ask your mother. It would be a big responsibility and most of the work would fall on her. I must discuss this with her."

Then Jim turned his attention back to the doctor. "How long will he be in the hospital?"

"It looks like his heart has decided to beat irregularly. It happens sometimes. We will be taking him to surgery for a pacemaker. It's not a serious surgery, so we expect him to make a full recovery. We will keep him here for about a week before he is ready to leave."

"What's a pacemaker?" Bidu asked.

The doctor explained all about the heartbeat and how sometimes it gets off the beat. A pacemaker would just help his heart to beat more in rhythm... sort of like the beat to a song. He tried to reassure her that Mr. Mayer would make a full recovery. Then he gave his card to Jim.

"I understand you have some talking to do and some decisions to make. Once you have talked it over, please give me a call so we can make the appropriate arrangements for Mr. Mayer. He's on his way to surgery now. I will call you once the procedure is complete.

You can go home and relax. Try not to worry. He will be fine and I'm sure he will be happy to have company when he is ready."

"All right," Jim answered. "Bidu, let's go home."

****

Bidu was happy to get home. She felt like she had been on quite a whirlwind of adventures and although she missed Piru and Lucinda, she was now more worried about Mr. Mayer and how she could help him.

She could smell wonderful aromas coming from the kitchen. Her mama was a fantastic cook and Bidu hadn't realized how hungry she was until now!

"What's for dinner, Mama?" she asked.

"Tonight we're having meatloaf and mashed potatoes, but first come give me a big hug. I've missed you so."

Bidu loved her parents. Her mother was the sweetest woman on the planet and her father was always so calm and kind. She loved her family and the comfort of her house. It felt good to be back.

"Bidu, how about you go and get cleaned up for dinner so I can talk with your mother for a bit?"

"OK, Daddy," said Bidu as she headed to her room. She took her time to wash up for dinner. She changed into her favorite pink and maroon robe. Then she laid on her bed to just relax until her parents called her.

It had only been about fifteen minutes when she heard her father call her name. She went right into the kitchen. She loved the little table that her mother always had set in a special way. Bidu loved the different table cloths and how her mother always had fresh flowers in the prettiest vases.

"Bidu, I'm so sorry to hear about Mr. Mayer," said her mother. "You did a good thing finding him and getting him to the hospital."

"Thanks, Mama. You know he doesn't have any family anymore."

"Yes, Bidu. Your father has been telling me all about it. We have decided that we would like Mr. Mayer to come here to recuperate."

"Oh yes!" cried Bidu. "I will take care of him and read to him."

"Take it easy, Bidu," said her mother, smiling. "I know you will want to be a great nurse and friend, but he will need a lot of time to rest as well. I like your idea about him staying in Grandma's room. She would be happy that the room is being used to help someone."

"Mama, I'm so happy. And I'm so hungry! That meatloaf smells amazing."

"Well then, let's eat and then we can talk about the plans once your father talks with the doctor. Deal?"

"Deal!" said Bidu as she began to gobble down the delicious dinner.

The phone rang just as they were finishing up their meal. Jim got right up to answer it. Bidu held her breath. She hoped it was information about Mr. Mayer. She could tell by what her father was saying that it must be the doctor.

"Yes, this is Jim. How is he doing? Oh, good, very good. Bidu will be happy to hear that."

Jim winked at Bidu and gave her a thumbs up that everything was OK. Bidu smiled back. She was very happy.

"Yes, Doctor. We can come tomorrow to talk about it, but I have spoken with my wife and we would really like to have Mr. Mayer come here to recuperate."

Now Bidu was standing up and giving thumbs up with both thumbs!

"Yes, Doctor. We will see you tomorrow. Thank you for calling."

Jim looked at his daughter. "Well, it's all set. Mr. Mayer will be coming here in five days. Until then, he will be resting at the hospital until they are sure everything is OK. We can go to see him tomorrow."

"Mama!" cried Bidu. "What do we need to get the room ready for Mr. Mayer?"

"I actually think the room is just fine, Bidu. It's very comfy and your grandma was so happy there."

Bidu thought she saw a tear welling up in her mama's eye.

"I miss Grandma," said Bidu.

"Oh, so do I," said her mother. "So do I. It will be nice to have someone here who needs our help."

Bidu nodded. She was so happy that Mr. Mayer would be coming. They all went into the living room to relax together as Bidu told them stories of her journeys. Her parents loved hearing every detail, but they were surprised to hear about all that had happened to their little girl on her adventures. They talked for hours until finally Jim said, "I think we need to call it a night! We can talk more tomorrow. We have to meet with the doctor at 10 o'clock and that will be here before we know it. Go get into bed, Bidu and we'll be right there to tuck you in."

Bidu got ready for bed and nestled into the big pink comforter that her mother had made for her. It was so soft and cuddly. She loved it when her parents came to tuck her in. It meant hugs and cuddles. She felt like tonight there would be big hugs and cuddles because they were all so happy to be together again.

The sun was shining through Bidu's window and the birds were chirping extra loudly that morning. Bidu looked at the clock. She saw that it was almost eight o'clock. She jumped out of bed to find her parents sitting having their coffee.

"Good morning, sweetheart," said her mother. "Can I get you something to drink? A hot chocolate maybe?"

"Yes, Mama. That sounds wonderful. Can I have it with 'mishmarshalls' too?"

They all laughed at the wonderful memories of the girls' first hot chocolate experience.

They talked and talked until it was time to get ready to go to meet the doctor. Bidu was looking forward to visiting Mr. Mayer. She couldn't wait to tell him the plan.

When they arrived at the hospital, they first went to meet with the doctor to find out all about Mr. Mayer's condition. The doctor was very happy with the pacemaker and he felt that Mr. Mayer would be as good as new in a very short time. They discussed the care he would need after he left the hospital. Jim assured the doctor that Mr. Mayer would get the best care possible between Marie and Bidu. The doctor seemed very comfortable with that. He escorted Bidu and Jim to Mr. Mayer's room.

"Mr. Mayer, you have some very special visitors," he said.

Mr. Mayer looked up and saw Bidu and Jim. "Hi there, you two. It's nice to have some company."

"Wow, Mr. Mayer," said Bidu. "You look great!"

"Well, I feel pretty good, all things considered," he said.

"The doctor told me that you found me in the shop, Bidu. And that you saved my life. Thank you, sweet girl."

"I'm just happy you're OK," Bidu answered.

"Daddy, tell Mr. Mayer the plan."

"What plan is that?" asked Mr. Mayer.

Jim put his arm around his daughter as he spoke to Mr. Mayer. "Bidu and I, and Marie too, would like to invite you to come to our house to rest and recuperate. We have a very special room all ready for you."

Mr. Mayer looked surprised. "I thought I might be going to a care facility, but your house sounds so much nicer." He smiled at Bidu. "Are you responsible for this too?"

Bidu just smiled. She really liked Mr. Mayer. He was so nice all the time, even when he was in the hospital.

"Then it's all set," said Bidu as she thought she saw Mr. Mayer's eyes fill with tears. He sure seemed happy with this arrangement and so was Bidu.

The five days went by quickly, and soon the day to bring Mr. Mayer home arrived. Of course, when he entered the house, he commented right away on the wonderful smells coming from the kitchen.

"Hello, Mr. Mayer," said Marie. "We are so happy to have you here. I hope you like to eat because I sure like to cook!"

"Oh, yes! I miss my wife and her home cooking. Thank you so much for having me."

Jim took Mr. Mayer to get him settled into his room. No one had stayed there since Bidu's grandma had passed away, but they were all happy they had a visitor now.

Mr. Mayer was supposed to stay for two weeks to rest and recuperate. He enjoyed every day and the time seemed to pass so quickly. He enjoyed sitting out on the porch every afternoon, sharing stories with Bidu about Gregor and all of the adventures he'd had with him. Bidu couldn't wait to hear his stories each day. She had lots of questions, but the first thing she asked him on the very first day they were on the porch was about how he found Gregor. It was her favorite story.

"Please tell me, Mr. Mayer, how did you meet Gregor?"

"Well, it's a very interesting story, Bidu. My wife, Elsie, and I were traveling in Greece. We met a very old woman who was amazing at telling fortunes. We sat at her table and for the first few minutes, she just stared at us and said, 'Uh huh, mmm' and made some other funny sounds. It was almost like she was in a trance. Then she looked at Elsie.

'My dear, you have some spiritual powers. I can feel them… and I can feel you. I believe the spirits have led you here. You may not understand this, but I have been waiting for you. I can't leave this world until I take care of one thing.'

'What is it?' Elsie asked.

The old woman continued. 'I have a very prized possession, but I am getting old now, and I need to find a home for him before I can leave this world. It can't just be any home. It has to be just the right home. I have no family, so I need to find the right soul. He needs care, but not very much. He can transport you to the past and to the future. He can take you on journeys that others can only imagine or dream about.'

'Oh my,' said Elsie. 'I can see this is very important for you. How can we help?'

The old woman reached under her table. She pulled out a purple velvet bag. She took the clock out of the bag and kept telling her story.

'This looks like a funny clock. It is a clock, but it's an enchanted clock with very special powers. It has been in this world since the beginning of time. His name is Gregor. He has had many masters. He never gets older, but we do. He cannot go on without a trusted master. He has been passed on many times. I have had him for over 40 years now. We have had many amazing adventures. It's time for me to pass him on to a new and trusted master so that he can live on.'

She paused for a minute and just looked at Elsie. Their eyes met and it was like they both knew something.

'Yes, yes, I think you are the one,' the old woman said.

'I think I am too,' said Elsie. 'I have had this exact dream many times. That's why I told my husband that we needed to come to Greece. I knew something would happen here.'

'And I, my dear, have stayed in this world because I knew you would be coming, and now you are here.'"

Mr. Mayer stopped talking. He seemed to get very emotional.

"What's wrong, Mr. Mayer?" Bidu asked in her softest voice.

"Nothing really, Bidu. It's just that when I think of Elsie and her goodness, I miss her so much. It was such a happy day for her when we found Gregor."

"Please tell me more," Bidu said. She wanted to know everything. "Did you take him that day? Did Gregor want to go?"

Mr. Mayer smiled and then went on. "When Gregor trusts his master, then he trusts that the master will find a new home for him that he can also trust. The old woman talked to him about it while Elsie and I sat silently. Gregor felt that Elsie was indeed the right one. He was ready and willing to go on. He loved the old woman, but he knew that he would always have to move on to a new master because he would never die. Once the old woman felt that Elsie was the right master, and Gregor felt it too, the old woman spent hours telling Elsie and I all about what Gregor could and couldn't do and all the best ways to care for him. She told Elsie how to program him, and how to communicate with him. If she had forgotten anything, she was sure that Gregor would be able to guide Elsie. After a while, the old woman said, 'I'm getting very tired. I think it's time that you take Gregor and go.' She held Gregor for another few minutes and spoke with him in her mind. We never knew what they said to each other. We never asked."

"I guess it's a good thing that you had a clock shop, right?" asked Bidu.

Mr. Mayer chuckled. "I didn't have the clock shop way back then. But having Gregor made me want to learn about all kinds of clocks. I started collecting them. As you know, I have many unusual clocks, but I have never found another one like Gregor. Elsie included me in so many of their adventures, and when she got sick, she and Gregor decided that I would become his new master. He didn't want to leave the shop and I was happy to have him because he eased the pain of losing my wife."

"That's the best story I have ever heard," said Bidu.

"Yes, Bidu, that is one of my favorite stories too."

As the days went by, Mr. Mayer shared so many wonderful stories and adventures with Bidu, but the story of how he and Elsie met Gregor was always her favorite. She could listen to it over and over without ever getting tired of hearing it.

Of course, he also wanted to know all about the adventures Bidu had been on and he enjoyed listening to Bidu's stories too. They developed a wonderful friendship and they grew to love each other very much.

Mr. Mayer became stronger every day. Marie cooked wonderful meals for him. Bidu went on walks with him every day so he could regain all of his strength. In the afternoons, when lunch was over, they shared stories together. It was truly a special time. But the day came that he no longer needed care. As the doctor promised, he did get to be as good as new. He had loved his time with Bidu and her family, but he knew it was time for him to go back home and he did want to get back to his shop. He so loved being around all of the clocks.

"Oh no!" cried Bidu, when he suggested it was time for him to go. "I love you being here. And I love all of your stories. Please don't go."

"Now, don't worry, Bidu," said Mr. Mayer as he took her hand in his. "I'm not very far away at all. I appreciate all your family has done for me and knowing you has been a great blessing and joy in my life. Please come to visit me as much as you like, and I will come to visit you too."

Marie and Jim heard Bidu talking with Mr. Mayer. They would miss him too, but they did understand that it was time for him to go.

"How about we have a standing date every Friday night for you to join us for dinner?" asked Marie.

"Oh, that sounds wonderful!" said Mr. Mayer. "I wouldn't miss it for the world. Thank you so much for everything."

"It has been our great pleasure," said Jim as Marie and Bidu nodded. Bidu ran over to him and gave him a big, long hug. He kissed her on the top of her head, just like her grandma used to do.

"Well, I better get my things. I think it's time to get going."

With that he went inside to pack up as Bidu and her parents sat on the porch.

"I'm so sad that he's leaving," said Bidu.

"I know, sweetheart. But he's not really going too far away and we will be seeing lots of him. You can go visit any time you want and he will be coming every week for a nice family dinner. So, nothing to feel so bad about, right?"

Bidu nodded yes, and she did understand, but still she felt sad.

Mr. Mayer came out with his bag all packed to say goodbye. There were more hugs and then Bidu walked him to the end of the walkway, and all the way down the street until he had to turn left to go to his house.

"Bye bye for now, sweet girl. I will see you soon."

He gave her one more hug, then blew her a kiss. She blew it back and then turned to walk back to her house.

When she got home, her parents were waiting at the door. They were both smiling.

"Your mother and I have an idea. Why don't we all take a nice bike ride to the lake together. We can pack a picnic and just enjoy being together."

"That's a great idea," said Bidu. They always seemed to know what to suggest to make her feel better.

"Go and get changed and I'll get the bikes ready."

"OK, Daddy. You got it!"

As Bidu walked into her room, she noticed the purple bag on her bed. On top of the purple bag was a letter. She sat on the edge of her bed and carefully opened the letter. She held back her tears as she read what it said:

Dear Sweet Bidu,

I'm not sure you realize how much knowing you has meant to me. You have been pure joy. I really never thought I would smile again after I lost my dear Elsie, but you have not only made me smile, you have made me laugh and feel love again. Just like the old woman who gave Gregor to Elsie, it's been time for me to start thinking of a new master for Gregor too. I have spoken with him and he agrees with me, that you are the one. You are young and you will have many more years and adventures with him. You will be a good and loving master. I know your heart and I know you will always only try to do good. Watch out for him. Protect him. He will always watch out for you and protect you as well. He will tell you amazing stories of his journeys. Now you can go whenever you want to see Piru and Lucinda and you can even go see the Alicorns again. There will be so many new wonderful adventures waiting for you. I hope you will come and sit with me on my porch and share them all with me as I have with you.

I wish you peace, blessings, love and a magical life.

Mr. Mayer

Bidu had tears streaming down her face. She felt the love and trust that Mr. Mayer had for her and she would never betray that. And she already felt close to Gregor. She was so happy to be looking at a life with him by her side.

"Gregor?"

"Yes, Bidu, my new master, how may I serve you?"

"I just want you to know how happy I am that you will be with me always. And I want to be sure that you are happy about it too."

"Yes, Bidu. I am very happy. I have had many masters, most have been good, some have been exceptional, and a few not so good. I believe that you will be the best one. I will tell you stories of all of my masters. I will take you on amazing adventures where we can do good. That is what I live for… and I believe as I know you now, that you want that too."

"Oh yes, Gregor. We are the same."

"So, my new master, what is your first wish?"

"Oh Gregor, I have so many wishes!"

"Well, why not start making a list and we will do them all!"

Gregor chuckled. Bidu giggled. She held him close and felt him near her. She couldn't help thinking about all the many amazing things that were about to happen...

Acknowledgments

I'd like to thank my parents, who raised me in a loving, calm, happy home which allowed my creative mind the freedom to be expressed!

My angel daughter, Holland, who continues to be my muse from the other side.

My family and friends, for their support and encouragement.

Bidu and Jove, my two amazing grandchildren who inspire me daily.

Gary, for supporting me and allowing me all the time I need to write!

Leslie, for helping me through the self-publishing maze.

Amanda, for reading every word and letting me tell her all my stories!

Grosvenor House Publishing, for holding my hand through the entire publishing process.

Lyn Stone, for her amazing, loving cover artwork.

About the Author

Denise Ganulin has been a singer/songwriter for many years, performing her songs across the country. (Visit her at DeniseGanulin.com.)

This is her first book. It was inspired and guided by the "real" Bidu, her precious granddaughter.

Denise lost her only child, Holland, several years ago. Holland left behind the blessings of two amazing children who fill Denise's life with joy, love, and inspiration.

Watch for two more books currently in the works:

Jove's Magical Adventures
Bidu's Adventures ~ The Clock Master.